# Crossed Signals

*One  Couples Journey of Sexual Discovery*

This story is a work of fiction. Names, characters, places and incidents are products of the author's imagination or are used fictitiously. Any resemblance to actual places, events, persons living or dead, are entirely coincidental.

Photo Credit: © Can Stock Photo Inc. / mocker

ISBN-13: 978-0692273227
ISBN-10: 0692273220

Printed in the United States of America

Forelsket Press • Las Vegas, Nevada

# Also by J.W. Richard

A Cougar Falls:
*Stunning Consequences*

The Roles We Play:
*A Spank-tacular Tale*

*'Sex' is as important as eating or drinking and we ought to allow the one appetite to be satisfied with as little restraint or false modesty as the other.*

**– Marquis de Sade**

# Chapter One

Nate grabbed a bath towel out of the linen closet and headed toward the master bath. Cynthia was sitting at the desk in the spare bedroom she used as her office, on Facebook as usual. Her auburn hair was tied in a ponytail which barely reached her neck. Wearing a loose-fitting t-shirt and gym shorts, it was still obvious she was in decent shape for a woman approaching forty. He paused in the doorway until she realized he was standing there. She looked up from the computer.

"Showering?"

"Getting ready for you."

"Can't it wait until you get back?"

"It's already been five days and I'll be gone for four, that's too long."

His wife turned back to Facebook without a word as he continued on to the bathroom. Nate stripped his clothes off and turned on the shower. While the water heated up he looked at the image of himself being reflected by the mirror. A few extra pounds but nothing serious, though the love handles were a bit more pronounced. His hair was mixed with a little gray but at least he had it all, his pecs hadn't sagged – not too much anyway – and his ass didn't droop. He thought he should start working out again but there never seemed to be enough time. All in all he felt he looked okay for someone who just turned forty-three.

Nate stepped into the shower and quickly washed his hair and soaped up. He grabbed the shower gel and lathered up his cock and balls making sure they were exceptionally clean or Cynthia would complain. He quickly grew erect; he really needed to cum. He hadn't jerked off at all in the last few days and was ready to explode. He really wanted to fuck but Cynthia just wasn't into it anymore, hadn't been since she miscarried almost two years ago. At least she understood his needs and took care of him once a week, but rarely more than that. He turned the water off and used the towel to dry himself, still rock-hard. He slipped on his robe and headed down the hall.

Cynthia was still at the computer. He walked into the room and stood next to her and let his robe fall open. She glanced over at him and his now semi-erect cock and turned back to her keyboard and hit a few keys. He went to the bed and propped himself up after tossing a pillow on the floor for her to kneel on. Cynthia finished what she was doing and knelt down in front of him with her hands on his thighs.

She took his cock in her right hand. "Did you wash it good?"

"It's squeaky clean."

"I hope so – it stunk last time."

"It didn't stink."

"You didn't have your nose in it. Trust me, it stunk."

"Well, it's clean now."

Cynthia sniffed his cock and then his balls. "Mmm, much better but make it quick, I've got things to do."

She licked up and down the shaft and worked her tongue around the head before slowly taking it in her mouth. She came up and went down a little quicker using her tongue as she went. Nate grew fully hard and focused on his cock in order to cum as fast as possible. It was the exact opposite of how it used to be. Back then he would think of other things to last as long as he could. Back when Cynthia liked giving him a blow job. Now if he didn't cum fast enough she would complain that her jaw hurt and stop. She picked up speed and he felt himself getting close.

She paused to take a breath. "Did you remember to pick up the dry cleaning?"

"Yes...come on, keep going."

She took him in her mouth again for a few seconds. "Don't forget to put the garbage out before you leave."

"I won't. C'mon..."

She started sucking again but stopped. "You're going down, I thought you needed it."

"If you'd stop talking to me and concentrate on what you're doing I wouldn't go down."

She stroked him and he started to stiffen again. "Hurry up, my jaw's starting to hurt."

Nate closed his eyes. He could feel his orgasm building again as she moved up and down. He was there. He felt his balls tighten. Almost. He started breathing heavier and Cynthia added some hand action since she knew he was close. He grunted and ejaculated into her mouth. It was nowhere near as intense as it should have been and was little more than a release. She got up and went to the bathroom where he could hear her spitting into the sink. She used to swallow. She returned with a washcloth and cleaned him up, handing him the cloth when she was done.

"Don't drip on the carpet."

She sat back at the computer as he got up. He came up behind her and gently kissed her on the neck. "Why don't you let me eat you?"

"I'm not clean."

"That doesn't bother me, I'll lick you clean."

"I'm just not into it today." She turned back to the computer screen.

# Chapter Two

Cynthia tossed her purse on the table by the front door and dropped her keys on the dish next to it. It was always the same when Nate when on one of his business trips – she missed his presence yet felt a sense of relief that he was gone. Planning to take it easy for the next four days, she would start with a long, relaxing bath. She went to her bedroom and stripped naked then headed to the bathroom to start the water, checked the balance of the hot and cold water as the tub filled and bubbles started rising.

While she waited she stepped on the scale – still holding at one-thirty-nine. One more pound and it would be time to start working out again. She wasn't totally satisfied with her shape but it didn't upset her either; her body could be more toned but at least with her five-foot-four-inch height she wasn't fat. Nate called her "soft" which he meant as a compliment because he didn't care for the hard-bodied type. Besides, he often told her, most of the weight was in her boobs. She looked in the mirror while cupping her breasts in her hands. She was lucky, so many women hated their breasts but she loved hers. Large enough to get attention without being out of proportion, her areolas were big, round and dark and reacted well to stimulation. Her fingers passed over her nipples and, on cue, they perked up and an electrical surge coursed through her body ending in her crotch.

Cynthia dipped a toe in to test the temperature then stepped in and slowly settled into the water. The bubbles covered her boobs as she put her head back and closed her eyes. She had relaxed almost to the point of falling asleep when she lightly started fingering her nipples. Lifting her right breast out of the water, she bent her head to reach it with her tongue. Sometimes, right before her period, she could get the nipple in her mouth and suck it. Not now though, the tongue barely touched the erect tip. Her hand let go and she settled back down under the bubbles. She spread her legs wide and lightly raked the inside of her thighs with her long fingernails causing her to shudder. Her left hand gently massaged her breasts while the fingers of her right ran through her pubic hair. She used her thumb and index finger to separate her labia and slowly inserted a finger into her vagina concentrating on the sensation as she moved in and out. She worked up to her now very swollen clit and rubbed, slowly picking up speed. After a few minutes she had a small orgasm followed by two or three more in quick succession. She wanted a big one but that would require the heavy artillery.

Cynthia opened the drain with her toe and hopped out of the bath. Grabbing the towel, she dried herself as she hurried to the bedroom and opened her nightstand drawer. She selected the largest of her three vibrators, lay down and spread her legs. She flipped the switch and heard a satisfying buzz as she immediately brought the tip against her clit. She shivered with pleasure, happy she hadn't lost the feeling, and went to work. This tool was about the same size as Nate – just over eight inches – and only a little thicker than he is. She brought it her mouth and sucked on it in to wet it, then put it between her legs. She pushed the tip into her vagina slowly, she was certainly lubricated enough, and went in as far as she comfortable with then worked it back and forth, in and out. She fingered her clit with her left index finger as the vibrator buzzed away. She had a small orgasm and turned over on her knees with her ass in the air and her face in the pillow and kept pumping away.

She could feel the big one coming. "Come on...come on........*Arrgghh... ahhhh....oh, yeah.*"

Totally spent, she collapsed on the bed and rolled on her side. She switched off the vibrator but left it inside her as she curled into a fetal position. She squeezed her legs together and felt the hard plastic of her toy. It didn't duplicate the feeling of Nate spooning her after he came with his cock still in her as he slowly went limp. Of course, that was back when they used to actually fuck. When he liked fucking her. They didn't fuck anymore and she knew why. *And it's my goddamn fault.*

Her ringing phone woke her. The vibrator had slipped out of her vagina and was underneath her. Cynthia pushed it aside and reached for the phone and checked the caller ID.

"Hey Kelly, what's up?"

"Just checking in. Did Nate leave?"

"Yeah, I dropped at the airport at lunchtime."

"So what are you going to do with yourself for three days?"

"Four days. I just took a bath and I'm just going to relax while he's away."

"Relax?" Kelly laughed. "You mean play with yourself. C'mon girl, let's do something."

"I'm just not into it."

"Cyn, I'm starting to worry about you. You never want to do anything. Let's have dinner."

"I really don't..."

"A drink then. Let's do happy hour tomorrow – it'll do you some good. You can play with yourself when you get home."

Cynthia laughed. "Okay, but just for a little while."

# Chapter Three

The shuttle stopped in front of the hotel. Nate retrieved his bag, tipped the driver and headed inside. He scanned the lobby looking for anybody he might know, seeing no one he proceeded to the desk and checked in. After completing the paperwork he found the elevator and went up to the eighth floor. The room was a decent size with a king bed and a refrigerator, but nothing out of the ordinary. He put away his clothes and stripped down to his underwear intending to watch TV or maybe take a short nap. He would go down to the hotel bar late in the afternoon hoping to meet up with a colleague or two before dinner.

The trip to Overland Park had been uneventful. Cynthia dropped him at the airport where he had enough time before his flight for a burger and a beer. He boarded on time and arrived in Kansas City twenty minutes ahead of schedule. His luggage didn't get lost, the shuttle was waiting and the thirty mile ride to his hotel didn't encounter any traffic. In short, he wasn't overly tired; he just wanted to put his feet up and relax a bit. He lay on the bed and turned on the television and scanned through the channels. There was nothing worth watching so he briefly considered hitting the porn channel but his company was paying the bill and might notice the charge so he just shut the TV off.

He closed his eyes and his mind wandered. As his thoughts drifted his cock hardened so he slipped his hand in his shorts and lightly rubbed it. He thought of Cynthia's half-hearted blow jobs and recalled the way it used to be. Back when she actually liked sucking his dick. Back when she enjoyed sex. Back when the two of them were really *in* love. He still loved her and believed she loved him, but he didn't feel like they were really *in* love anymore. He didn't think a miscarriage did this to all women – certainly not for this long. Would it ever be like those early days when they were newly in love and deeply in lust? Would they ever be like that again?

The first time she sucked him off was a mind-blowing experience to say the least. They had been on a number of dates. At first they only made out. It was like they were teenagers all over again even though she had just turned thirty. Then came the day in the park where she jerked him off outdoors at the lake on a blustery, early December day. That was followed by another hand job in the car after a date a couple of weeks later, but they still hadn't fucked and she hadn't let him go any further than a hand up her shirt. She told him she had a few prior boyfriends but he was beginning to wonder if she might still be a virgin. Then came the party on New Year's Eve. *That party.*

They were at her friend Kelly's house with about a dozen other couples and a few assorted singles of both sexes. As midnight approached most people weren't feeling any pain and quite a few, including Cynthia, were pretty well hammered. The crowd counted down the seconds and shouted "Happy New Year" in unison and kissed their partners and each other. Cynthia locked lips with him and buried her tongue down his throat. To this point she had been quite reserved in front of others but not this time. His hard-on was obvious to anyone who might be looking – Cynthia was certainly aware of it as she looked down at it and smiled. She took his hand and, in an inebriated zigzag, led him into the deserted kitchen.

She let out a drunken giggle and pulled him into the walk-in pantry and pulled the door shut leaving them in darkness. He went to kiss her – which is what he thought she wanted – but she pushed him away. Instead she dropped to her knees and unbuckled his belt, opened his pants and lowered the zipper. She pulled his slacks and underwear down to his knees exposing his very erect and throbbing cock. She grabbed it with her right hand and without hesitation put him in her mouth. She worked his cock like a master, with her tongue and lips as she slowly moved up and down taking him as deep as she could. It was warm, wet, and pure ecstasy. He couldn't remember ever being sucked so well. He tried to hold back but couldn't as he felt his orgasm starting. He turned his head to the side so he could bite his shirt collar to keep from crying out. Instead he grunted and unleashed a huge load into her mouth. She kept sucking his cock until she had swallowed every last drop as he slowly went flaccid. Cynthia stood up. She pulled his underwear and slacks back up, zippered them and fastened his belt while he leaned back against the shelves trying to catch his breath.

She stood on her toes and put her lips by his ear and whispered, "Take me home and fuck the living shit out of me."

She opened the pantry door and the light flooded in. He was speechless when he saw the kitchen was packed, everyone had crowded in. Then they started to applaud wildly and a few held up their glasses in a toast. Cynthia smiled as she held up her clenched fist in triumph as she made her way through the kitchen. He quickly realized three things: first, she was no virgin; second, she told someone what she planned to do so she wasn't nearly as reserved or prudish as he thought; and third, she was going to be one wild ride so he better hang on tight. *Where had that woman gone? Was the change his fault somehow?*

# Chapter Four

The Rabbit Hole Tavern was fairly busy as usual for a Friday but Cynthia and Kelly still managed to find seats together at the bar. They'd polished off a flatbread pizza and order of mozzarella sticks to go along with their drinks. Kelly was one of those slightly chubby, always bubbly, talkative women that were either a joy to be around or a total pain in the ass with their perpetual happiness. Cynthia tried to catch her mood but it wasn't working despite being on her third raspberry martini.

They'd chatted about their respective parents and Kelly updated her on every detail of her two kids and husband Doug. Every time her friend asked about her life Cynthia deflected to conversation back to Kelly. There just wasn't much to talk about. Nate was doing very well at his job but she wasn't doing much of anything and talked about going back to work but it never seemed to happen. She'd toyed with the idea of returning to school but the thought didn't excite her at all. Putting in a few of applications at the mall never resulted in a job. They didn't need the money but she did need something to do with herself besides play with her clit. Kelly was only half-joking about her always playing with herself. She masturbated every day, usually several times as long as Nate wasn't home.

Cynthia scanned the bar. There were more men than women, mostly business types. A few glanced their way and she saw one obviously checking out Kelly. Her friend may be married but she liked to look sexy when she went out. Her blouse, as usual, was open one button too far and the black lace of her bra was visible along with a generous helping of cleavage. Her theory was that if you show something up front they won't notice an ass that was a bit too big in the back. Cynthia glanced surreptitiously down at her own boobs. She was a bit larger than Kelly but wasn't revealing much which was good because she had no desire to attract attention. She resumed scanning the length of the bar.

Kelly followed her gaze. "See something you like."

"Just watching a guy check you out."

"Is he hot?" Kelly tried to swivel her head around.

"Does it matter? You *are* married."

"I am and it does. I want to know I've still got it."

Cynthia laughed. "Well you are half naked."

"Whatever it takes." Kelly cocked her head sideways and looked at her. "Was that a laugh I heard?"

"It's the martinis talking."

"Well then get another one; it's about time you loosened up."

Cynthia drained her glass and held it up to signal the bartender for another drink. She was passed her limit and was certainly feeling the alcohol, but she needed it. Kelly had been right, she had to get out. She was in a major rut and needed to do something about it. What that was she had no idea.

Kelly, feeling her drinks as well, snorted. "I am not."

"Not what?"

"Half naked. I'm simply showing off my assets."

Cynthia laughed again as the bartender put a fresh drink in front of her and cleared away the plates from their food.

Kelly sipped her drink. "Don't you feel good when guys check you out?"

"Doesn't happen much anymore."

Kelly looked up and down the bar and then into the mirror behind the bottles. She looked at Cynthia then back to the mirror, then back down the length of the bar.

"Look at her – she's gorgeous," Kelly said.

Cynthia looked around. "Who? I don't see."

Kelly gestured to the mirror. "Look that way."

Cynthia looked in the mirror. "Where? I don't..."

"I'm looking at you. You're gorgeous and don't see it.

"I'm not..."

"Sweetie, sometimes I wish I was gay just so I could fuck you."

Cynthia laughed. "I tried that in college. Trust me, girls are way overrated."

Kelly drained her glass. "Take a good look at yourself. Half the guys in here would take you home in a heartbeat."

"Only half?"

"That's it – the other half are mine!"

Kelly excused herself to go to the ladies room. Cynthia took another sip from her martini then slid it, still half-full, across the bar. She'd had enough. She paid the tab before Kelly returned, signed the credit card receipt and gave it to the bartender. Kelly would be pissed that she paid but she'd get over it. As she was putting her wallet away she noticed a guy walking toward her. Dark hair, muscular build, nice face and as he approached she noticed his blue eyes. When he and stopped at her chair her heart skipped a beat.

"Hi, I'm Zach. I noticed you were about to leave and I was hoping you'd stay a little longer and let me buy you a drink."

"Thank you, but no." She held up her hand displaying her wedding band.

He smiled at her. "Some women just wear them to keep guys like me away."

"No, it's real."

He looked disappointed. "Well, have a great night then. I would've kicked myself for days if I let a beautiful woman like you leave without at least trying."

She stood up as Kelly returned. "Well thanks. You have a great night too."

Zach smiled at her. "Hope to see you again sometime."

She started walking toward the door and motioned for Kelly to follow. As they were going through the door Kelly turned to look at the guy she had been talking to and then back at her with a puzzled look.

"Who the hell was *that*?"

"Some guy practicing his pickup lines."

"They don't check you out anymore, huh? I told you you're still hot."

Cynthia smiled. As they walked to their cars she thought of Zach and his blue eyes. She wondered what his cock was like as she tried to decide which vibrator she was going to use when she got home.

# Chapter Five

Nate woke from his short nap. The hard-on he rubbed while falling asleep was still there so he took it in his hand and stroked slowly then gradually increased his tempo. This is what he thought of as a "maintenance jerk" meant to get a load out so he wouldn't be walking around all evening with an erection. As he picked up the pace as he felt himself starting to cum. He closed his eyes, expelled a large breath and ejaculated several inches into the air with his semen settling onto his stomach and dripping over his hand. After he settled down he made his way to the bathroom and cleaned up.

He showered and changed before heading down to the bar for a cocktail. He saw a few people from his company but no one he knew well. There was a baseball game on the bar television while he had some dinner and a few more drinks. By ten that night he still hadn't seen anyone he cared to talk to so he went up to his room to with the intention of getting a good night's sleep. He called home to say goodnight to Cynthia. He had obviously awakened her so he just told her he'd arrived safely and that she should go back to bed.

The next morning Nate was at the company breakfast before the first of several scheduled meetings. He made a plate at the buffet and carried, along with a coffee, to an empty table. He saw his friend Marc scooping some eggs and piling on the bacon so he signaled for him to come over and join him.

"I was looking for you at the bar last night," Nate said.

Marc took a sip of coffee. "Would've loved to be there. My flight was delayed and I didn't get in until after one in the morning."

"You do look a little rough around the edges."

"Tell me about it. I'd be asleep by the morning break if I wasn't presenting...I might be asleep *while* I present."

"I feel your pain. Dinner tonight?"

"I plan on taking a nap for dinner but we can hit the bar later. Getting seriously hammered is on the agenda; I can sleep through tomorrow's meetings."

"Sounds like a plan."

Later that night Nate and Marc were at the *Sly Fox*, a bar within walking distance of the hotel. Marc was a regional director of sales whose role was to oversee area sales managers. Technically that made Marc Nate's boss but they started with the company at the same time and even went through company training together almost ten years ago. The two of them were best of friends and Marc's superior position in the corporate hierarchy had never been an issue. Nate had been in the running for the position Marc held but made it known that he didn't want it because it would have meant relocating. Cynthia was reluctant to move away from her friends and family so he withdrew from consideration. The way Cynthia has been lately he often wondered if that had been a mistake. Moving might have been a good thing for her.

Nate and Marc drank beer, played pool, drank beer, played darts, drank beer. They ate some nachos, drank beer and drank even more beer. The place attracted a good size crowd and at the beginning of the night there had been quite a few people from his company. Now that it was approaching midnight there were the two of them and a group of three women at the other end of the bar left from his firm though the place was still full of people. Nate looked around and noticed that the age of the crowd got younger with each passing hour and now he was one of the oldest people left.

The two of them talked about Marc's life and how things were going since he got divorced a couple of years ago. He played more golf and did things he never had time for while married. He saw his two kids regularly and had a cordial relationship with his ex – as long as he paid alimony and child support on time. He dated a few women here and there but it was mostly one night stands with assorted lonely ladies. Being divorced, he said, sucked the big one as did dating again in his mid-forties.

Marc swiveled his stool toward Nate. "So, how's Cindy?"

"Cynthia, she hates being called Cindy."

"She's not here."

Nate changed the subject and gestured toward the group of women. "Who's that one there, is she new?"

"I assume you're referring to the gorgeous one built like a brick shithouse."

"That's the one, the other two I recognize."

"Tamara Reynolds, sales manager of the Tampa office. Great resume so I hired her two months ago."

"Resume? Let me guess, thirty-eight D and a total airhead."

"Close – they're double-D; she's thirty-seven-years-old but certainly no airhead. She has a degree in accounting and has won several major sales awards at her previous firm. Single, never married and in addition to being good looking and having a killer body, she has a great personality."

"So you mean you actually hired her for her *qualifications*? That's a switch."

"I did try to give her my personal "breathalyzer" test but she wouldn't bite."

"Probably said that thing in your pants was way too small to give an accurate reading."

"Funny. Truth is she's the best hire I ever made."

"Certainly not bad to look at," Nate said.

The bartender put down a couple of fresh beers. Nate took a sip while getting a good look at Tamara. She had an easy laugh as she chatted with her colleagues. Medium brown hair in a layered cut, full lips, classic nose, brown eyes and very, very pretty. She was sitting down but her boobs were impressive and, he was sure, natural. What he could see of her ass showed it to be fairly small for someone with such big breasts. He would love to see her in a bikini. He wondered if she shaved her pubic hair and hoped she didn't. Then he wondered why it matters because he'll never see her pussy anyway. He was snapped out of his reverie by Marc saying something.

"Huh?"

"I said, you never answered me about Cindy...Cynthia. How is she?"

Nate hesitated a moment. "She's fine."

"Fine? Fine? Holly shit, what's wrong?"

"What? Nothing."

"Fine is what people say when things are really fucked up. Then there's the way you said it, which tells me something's bothering you. What is it?"

"Nothing...it's just..."

Marc took a big gulp of beer. "Come on, out with it."

"It's just, well...things have changed since her miscarriage."

"That was like, what, three years ago?"

"Not quite two."

"She should be over it by now. How has she changed?"

"She's lost interest in sex."

"Cindy?"

"Cynthia."

Nate had never shared that information with anyone and wasn't certain he should have but after so many beers it just slipped out. Though if he couldn't confide in Marc he couldn't trust anyone. If nothing else, his friend was discreet.

Marc shook his head. "My god, that woman was...we used to joke about having to knock really loud when we came over because you guys were probably fucking."

"These days you can walk in without ringing the bell."

"Wow. You don't get anything at all?"

"I get a half-assed – emphasis on half-assed – blow job once a week. I can't remember the last time we actually fucked ."

"She's totally lost it?"

"Totally, with me anyway. I do find her vibrator out every once in a while so at least she's not totally dead."

The surprise wouldn't leave Marc's face. "Didn't she have counseling after the miscarriage?"

"Yup, we both did. But the counselor was a moron. We would have been better off reading from a text book."

"Do you talk about this?"

"Every time I try she shuts down so I just give her space. I'm hoping she'll come around. In the meantime I have huge calluses."

Marc touched Nate's arm. "There are plenty of hookers around the hotel."

"I don't want a hooker. I miss Cynthia, I miss her energy...she was insatiable."

Marc excused himself to hit the men's room. The trio of ladies got up to leave but they paused at the door. Tamara looked in his direction, said something to the other two and walked his way. She oozed raw sexuality and Nate understood why she won sales awards. She reached his stool and smiled.

She offered her hand. "Nate Kearns? I'm Tamara Reynolds."

Nate took her hand. "A pleasure to meet you."

"I've heard so much about you, I'm in a similar position to yours in the Tampa office."

"All lies I assure you."

Tamara laughed. "I was hoping we could have lunch tomorrow; I'd love to pick your brain since I'm fairly new here."

"It would be my pleasure. I'll look for you after the morning session."

"Great!"

He watched her walk away and felt himself getting hard. Back in hotel room he stripped naked, lay on the bed and stroked his cock. This wasn't maintenance. He did it slowly, fondled his balls, varied the pressure and took his time. His eyes were closed as he thought of Tamara. He imagined sucking on her nipples until she squirmed. In his fantasy she had dark, thick and neatly trimmed pubes and he thought of what her pussy must taste like. When he thought of slipping inside of her and he couldn't hold back anymore. His cock pulsated and semen shot out of him in great volume. When he finished he went to sleep without cleaning up. His dreams were pleasant that night.

# Chapter Six

Cynthia stretched as she woke on Saturday morning. Two of her vibrators were on the bed with her, remnants of the previous night's marathon buzz-fest. She opened the draw of her nightstand and put away the larger of the two. She switched on the smaller and set it to low as she spread her legs and vibrated herself to her morning orgasm. After she came she put her toy away, made the bed and went to the kitchen to brew some java. She was scooping coffee into the basket when the phone rang. She grabbed it thinking it might be Nate but the caller ID displayed Kelly's name.

"Hey Kelly, you're up bright and early."

"It is almost ten. I called to see if you were hung over."

"No, but I was feeling it last night."

"Want company for coffee?"

Cynthia looked at the clock. "Sure, give me thirty minutes."

She added a couple extra scoops, poured in the water and hit the "brew" button. She could smell the coffee as she threw off her nightshirt and jumped in the shower for a quick rinse. She lathered her pussy and lightly fingered her clit and was rewarded with a nice tingle but she stopped because she didn't have time. She'd finish later. She turned off the shower, quickly dried herself, threw on some shorts and t-shirt but no bra. and went back to the kitchen. She poured herself a coffee and set a cup out for Kelly. Her friend arrived a few minutes later holding a box of fresh pastries from the bakery.

Cynthia took the box. "You're trying to make me fat."

"Pudginess loves company."

Cynthia put the pastries on a plate and set them on the table. Kelly was a little chunky but nothing serious. A pretty face and a nice rack offset the few extra pounds and most guys probably thought she was sexy. Not that it mattered, she was married and not one to fool around, at least not as far as Cynthia knew and they did share everything. Almost. Cynthia did confide in her about how much she masturbated but not about her sex life, or lack thereof. She wanted to but never found the right moment.

"Last night was fun," Cynthia said.

"It was. You were right, I needed to get out."

Kelly chuckled. "I'm always right, remember that."

"You were right about something else too."

"Of course, what this time?"

Cynthia took a bite out of an apple turnover. "Mmm, this is so good. I was doing some research on the internet, as you suggested. I've come to the conclusion that you're right, I'm a masturbation addict."

"Well duh, you do it like twenty times a day."

"I'm not that bad."

"How many times today?"

"Only once, when I woke up."

"I prefer to do it once in a while before I go to sleep."

"I do it then too, but I do it almost every night."

"How many times a day are you playing with yourself?"

"I've been counting – one website said I should keep track – lately it's been at least three or four times a day, sometimes more."

"How do you get anything done?"

"I don't."

Kelly finished her coffee. "Isn't it affecting you sex life with Nate?"

Cynthia stood up and took both of their cups to the counter to pour more coffee. Kelly has given her openings like this before but she always let them pass. If she couldn't talk to her best friend who could she discuss it with? She trusted her completely so it was now or never.

Cynthia swallowed hard. "It can't affect what doesn't exist."

"Huh? I don't understand, what doesn't exist?"

"My sex life with Nate."

"What? The way you guys fucked rabbits couldn't keep up with you."

Cynthia could see by her friends' expression that she was truly shocked. Kelly just looked at her with her head tilted to one side until she finally found her voice.

"You don't do anything at all?" Kelly asked.

"I suck him off once a week or so but even that's mechanical."

"I...I don't believe this. When's the last time you actually fucked?"

When was the last time? She thought for a few moments before it came to her. They had been out to a movie and went for drinks afterward. They weren't drunk but they were feeling pretty good. Nate started kissing her when they got home, or tried to. She pushed him away and got ready for bed. When she returned to the bedroom he was on the bed, naked and erect. She figured she'd have to blow him before she could go to sleep so she just went for it. She took his cock in her hand and was about to put it in her mouth when he stopped her.

"I want to eat you," he said.

"No, I'm not clean."

"I don't care."

She protested some more but her just pushed her back and lifted the nightshirt over her head and tossed it aside. He nudged her and she lay back on the bed and spread her legs. He licked her thighs and slowly worked his way up to her clit. He had always been amazing at cunnilingus but this time she felt nothing, absolutely nothing. She did something she had never done with him or anyone else before – she faked it. She started squirming a little and breathing a little heavier. She moaned and let out a gasp and pulled him up. He slipped inside of her and started pumping slowly, then picked up his pace. She closed her eyes as he thrust and waited for him to finish, unable to pretend anymore. Finally he raised himself up, pushed in as deep as he could, grunted and came. She could feel the pulsations of his cock as he ejaculated into her vagina. He pulled out of her, rolled over and promptly fell asleep. She turned on her side, her back to him. She felt his semen oozing out of her and dripping down her leg and began to cry silently as she wondered what had happened to them. They hadn't fucked since.

"You didn't answer," Kelly said. "How long's it been?"

"I was thinking....seven months."

# Chapter Seven

Nate had trouble staying awake during the morning sessions but managed to get through them. He still had an afternoon and one more morning to get through before heading back home. The only thing keeping him going right now was the thought of lunch with Tamara. Though he jerked off thinking about her the night before any fantasies were alcohol fueled. He had never cheated on Cynthia despite numerous opportunities to do so and he certainly wasn't going to start now. That didn't mean he wasn't drawn to Tamara; she was, to use a highly technical term, smokin' hot.

The most convenient place for lunch was the hotel coffee shop. While they ate they compared notes about the company and how she was adjusting to her new role in the Tampa office. She quizzed him a little on how he handled various situations such as sales reps not meeting quota or letting their personal problems affect performance. They talked about how you made the transition from being in the field as part of the sales force to being on the management side. It was something he struggled with at first just as she seemed to be now. She may be gorgeous but she was dead serious about her job. He imagined that someone who looked like her had to prove herself in ways ordinary people didn't. He quickly got the impression that she was a woman used to getting her way and one who didn't take "no" for an answer.

"Being in sales was easy," Tamara said. "Most of my clients wanted to fuck me so they'd say yes. I never did of course, but I let them think it was possible if that's what they wanted to believe."

Nate was a bit shocked by her candidness and it must have showed.

"Don't act so surprised," she said. "I don't mean to sound like a narcissist, but I know how I look and I'm hit on constantly. The looks used to be a drag until I embraced it. Besides I'm sure you closed plenty of deals because women clients wanted to have sex with you."

Nate laughed. "Yeah right."

"I'm serious. Haven't you ever met a woman and wondered what it would be like to get her in bed?"

"Of course, but..."

"You probably even thought that about me."

Nate felt his face redden like an adolescent caught by his mother when he had his dick in his hand. He couldn't look at her and he played with the remnants of the Caesar salad on his dish. He eventually looked back up and she was smiling and staring right into his eyes. When his eyes made contact with her dark brown ovals she let out a laugh.

"I knew it. News flash – women think like that too, it's human nature. If you were selling to me I'd want to fuck you."

"I try not to think like that, I am married."

"You're still human. I bet Cynthia thinks like that too."

Nate's eyes widened and jaw dropped open. "How do you know my wife's name?"

"In sales you need to know your prospects."

"I'm one of your prospects?"

"Haven't decided."

Nate wasn't sure how to handle this. Yes, physically he'd love to have sex with her but he wasn't about to let that happen. Yet when she seductively licked her lips, her thick and luscious lips, he was instantly erect. He had to change the direction of this conversation, end lunch and avoid her until the conference was over. Easier said than done since she had totally mesmerized him. He would at least attempt to change the subject.

"So, how come you never married?"

Tamara grinned at him. "How do you know I never married? Have you been checking up on *me*?"

"Marc told me last night when I asked who you were."

She smiled as she twirled the ice in her water glass. "So you were asking about me, huh?"

"I noticed you at the bar...how could I not?"

"I'm flattered. Did he tell you about interviewing me for the job?"

"A little."

"He was drooling like an overeager puppy. Talk about guys wanting to fuck me; he had a hard-on during the entire interview...probably jerked off as soon as I left."

"Are you always this..."

"Potty-mouthed?"

"I was going to say forward."

"Only with people I'm comfortable with."

Tamara may be comfortable but he was uneasy. He caught a break when the waiter served coffee and asked if they wanted desert. He was relieved when she declined. He had successfully managed to steer the conversation away from him.

"You never answered my question," he said.

Tamara took a deep breath. "Marriage was in my grand plan when I was young. But I decided I didn't want kids so it wasn't as important, though my mother begs to differ. As far as guys, well let's say I can be a bit...demanding."

Nate laughed at that. "You don't say."

"Is it that obvious? Look, I'm in charge, especially in the bedroom. A lot of guys are fine with that, they like to be dominated."

"But?"

"But I want a guy who isn't a pussy, he needs to be firm and confident...but understand who's boss."

Nate had a vision of Tamara as a dominatrix and certainly didn't see himself as a submissive. He hoped she realized this but wanted to be sure.

"Well then, you can cross me off your prospect list."

Tamara looked directly into his eyes. "You see, you're forgetting who's boss."

"I already have a boss, as I said, I'm married."

"Relax, I joking with you."

The waiter came by and cleared their plates. He reached for the check but Tamara grabbed it and charged it to her room. Marc was right about one thing, this woman was no airhead. He enjoyed talking to her but he was somewhat intimidated by her – and intrigued.

She clutched her purse as she prepared to get up. "We should chat some more. Meet me at the *Sly Fox* tonight."

"I don't think I can."

"See, you're forgetting who's boss again. Shall we say seven? And dress casual, I know I will."

"But I don't..."

Tamara stood up and walked a step toward his chair. She put a hand on his shoulder and he felt a jolt of electricity at her touch. She leaned into him causing her blouse to billow open revealing the white lace of her bra and two succulent breasts trying to escape. He couldn't help but stare. She knew he was looking – just as she intended.

"You'll be there."

# Chapter Eight

Cynthia cleared away the coffee pot and placed the cups in the dishwasher. Kelly went to use the bathroom and when she returned they moved to the living room with Cynthia sitting in a leather chair and Kelly on the sofa next to her, kicking off her shoes and pulling her legs up under her. They agreed this was a day for a very long, and long overdue, talk. Cynthia explained that the sex stopped after the miscarriage and she only sucked him off as a form of maintenance so he wouldn't leave her for someone else. She knew he didn't want sex with her anymore but he didn't want a divorce either. During her recovery Nate became distant and she said it was obvious that he blamed her and she understood and agreed that it was her fault. As much as he blamed her, she blamed herself even more.

Kelly shook her head. "But that's ridiculous, why would he blame you? How could it be your fault?"

"Because I didn't listen. I developed very high blood pressure in my fifth month. I was placed on complete bed rest but I was going crazy."

"Still, I don't see how..."

"Let me finish. I kept doing things I shouldn't have to stay busy and keep from losing my mind. One day I collapsed...you may remember I had to go to the hospital."

"I remember," Kelly said.

"I was told again to stay off my feet as much as possible. I listened...for a while. After about two weeks I started feeling better and began overexerting myself again. That's when it happened."

"Still, it really isn't your fault. It's a sad thing that happens to a lot of people."

"My OB/GYN came to the emergency room, he was so angry with me. At first Nate was supportive. Then after a follow-up exam my doctor said the miscarriage had done a lot of damage and I probably wouldn't get pregnant again."

"Cynthia, I'm so sorry."

Cynthia wiped at her eyes. Kelly got up and found some tissues in the bathroom, came back and handed them to her. She dabbed her tears before continuing.

"You know how much Nate wanted a family," Cynthia said. "The look on his face hurt me worse than losing our baby. That was when I knew I lost him."

Kelly reached across and squeezed her hand. "Didn't you guys get counseling?"

"We did, it didn't help."

"Still, I'm sure Nate..."

"Damn it Kelly – he hasn't fucking touched me since then except when he's blind stinking drunk."

They kept talking for more than an hour. They cried, laughed, and cried some more. Kelly kept insisting that she and Nate go for counseling or, she feared, their marriage wouldn't survive. That, Kelly said, would be the biggest tragedy of all because she had never seen two people so ideally suited for one another. Cynthia knew her friend was right but she didn't know how to approach Nate. In truth, she was scared to death that a counselor would tell him to leave her. Kelly had to go home so she would be there before her kids got back from school and said she would call later. Cynthia went to the bedroom and masturbated.

Late in the afternoon she wakened from the sleep she'd fallen into after having an orgasm. Cynthia couldn't remember but thought it must have been a big one to go out like that. She went to the kitchen and rummaged around for something to make for dinner. She hadn't been to the grocery store in a week so there wasn't much in the house that appealed to her. Tomorrow would be shopping day to restock before Nate came home. A thought came to her and actually made her smile. She would treat herself by going out to eat, maybe starting with a drink. One of those raspberry martinis would hit the spot.

Cynthia stripped and sat down in front of the mirror to put on some makeup. She didn't need much and often went without it but today she wanted to feel her best. Next would be bra and panties, a matching pink lace set seemed right. She trimmed her black pubes a little before slipping the panties on and twisted herself around to check her ass in the mirror. Satisfied she fastened the bra but before slipping on the straps she cupped her boobs and turned side to side to look at their reflection. She pulled the straps up and settled the girls into the cups. Next she chose her stonewashed jeans and a white, button-down blouse. After putting everything on she looked in the mirror but wasn't quite satisfied. She stared at herself for a moment and then opened one button and spread the blouse a bit. She went to her jewelry box and chose a pendant that dangled between her breasts and added a matching bracelet and earrings. The last piece was her engagement ring which she placed next to her wedding band, she wanted to look good, not available. Now she was done.

She went to go to the *Rabbit Hole* again. The food's good, the raspberry martinis better, and feeling like an attractive woman the best. She didn't even masturbate first.

# Chapter Nine

The afternoon went by quickly with several meetings in rapid succession. Things wrapped up shortly after four and Nate was looking forward to a shower and short nap before dinner. He had no intention of going anywhere near the *Sly Fox* that evening. He looked for Marc in the hallways of the hotel's conference center and finally found him coming out of the men's room.

"Cocktails later?" Nate asked.

"I'd love to but I have a mandatory meeting for upper management, something you underlings wouldn't understand."

"I understand all too well. You pucker up and wander around from VP to VP kissing ass. Can't you skip it?"

Marc shook his head. "Not this time. We can meet for lunch tomorrow or hang at the airport bar while we wait for our flights."

"What time do you head out? My flight's at four," Nate said.

"That's good, mine's three-thirty. Hey, there's a bunch of sales people and managers heading out to dinner and then the Fox tonight, why don't you hang with them?"

"I think I'll skip it."

"Tamara will be there."

The shower and nap went as planned and Nate thought about staying in for a room service dinner and watching a movie in his room. The food on the menu wasn't to his liking so he rifled through a few of the brochures for local restaurants that he found in the drawer. He read one for an Italian place that looked appealing at it was only a couple of blocks away so he decided to eat there. He put on his jeans and a polo shirt and headed out.

The eatery was casual dining and it wasn't quite six so there weren't a lot of people there. He ordered a veal dish and a glass of wine telling the waiter to take his time. He enjoyed his meal at a leisurely pace but was still done in less than an hour. He started walking back to the hotel and looked in to a couple of the bars he passed but they weren't his kind of crowd so he kept moving. He was passing the Sly Fox and looked in without entering. He didn't see any people from his company, they were probably still out a dinner. Nate decided it would be safe to go in and have a quick beer and then head back to his room for the night.

It was well past seven and still no one from his firm had shown up. Nate thought they may have gone somewhere else so he ordered another beer while he watched the rest of a game show on the television. He was about halfway through and planning to leave as soon as he finished when a group walked in. They were from his company and several people waved at him as they entered and one suggested he join them. He declined but there was no sign of Tamara so he ordered another beer thinking she must have gone elsewhere. No sooner had the bartender set the glass down in front of him she walked in with the two women she had been with the night before. She looked his way but was obviously heading toward the group that had moved to the rear of the bar.

Tamara winked as she passed. "Told you."

Nate watched as she walked by and most every head in the place turned to follow her as well. Her idea of casual was impressive to say the least. A form hugging top that highlighted her perfectly shaped, and very large, breasts and jeans so tight they seem to have been form-fitted around her. Her ass was flawless and if someone said she was a past Playmate of the Year no one would doubt it. She accessorized with earrings a bracelet and matching gold necklace and finished the look with a narrow silk scarf tied around her neck.

Her sexiness was as subtle as a brick wall. She carried herself with ease and exhibited such a confident and graceful manner that must have enthralled guys everywhere she went.

He watched her as she talked with the group. All eyes were on her but they way she interacted indicated that she was interested in everyone else and had no desire to be the center of attention. He looked at himself in the mirror. He was casual, well groomed and, compared to her, bland. Though he still told himself he wasn't interested in her, he wondered why in the world a woman like that would even be remotely interested in him. The game show had switched to a sports highlight program and he gave it his attention – or tried to. He felt a light tap on the shoulder as one of the women from Tamara's group asked him to join them. Not wanting to be rude, he followed her over.

There were eight others, a mix of men and women, most of them fairly new to the company. He was quickly included in the conversation about sales tactics and they listened intently to what he had to say. He was speaking by rote, sharing tips he usually gave when he ran his own meetings for his team. Though it was old hat for him, it probably was new to them. He watched Tamara as he talked. She barely acknowledged him and never looked directly at him and he began to wonder if he'd upset her in some way. About thirty minutes and a beer and a half later he excused himself and went back to the bar.

Not long after he sat back down Nate felt a presence and heard the stool next to him scrape against the floor. He glanced over just as Tamara was sitting down. She held up an empty glass for the bartender and watched him as he prepared her drink. When he put it down she leaned forward and said something to him. He came back with two shot glasses and poured from a bottle of Jose Cuervo. Tamara picked up one glass and pushed the other toward him.

She raised the glass. "Drink."

"I don't do shots."

"Just one – drink."

He looked at her and slowly picked up the shot. They clinked glasses and downed it in one gulp. He felt it burn as it went down and did his best not to grimace. She licked her lips in appreciation and put the glass down. Nate put his next to hers and pushed them both across the bar. The bartender looked at him and he shook his head "no." One was certainly enough for him.

Tamara turned her stool to face him. "Sorry I ignored you there, had to pay attention to my guys."

"Oh, I didn't notice."

"Then why were you sulking when you came back here?"

"I wasn't sulking, I just had enough of sales talk."

She laughed. "You were sulking."

Nate looked at her, she was absolutely right. He wanted her attention despite trying to fool himself into thinking he didn't care. He looked at her face and for the first time notice tiny wrinkles by the corners of her mouth and the start of crow's-feet by the eyes. To him it indicated experience and only made her seem sexier, as if that were possible. His nose picked up the subtle scent of her perfume and wondered how it would taste if he nibbled on her neck. He felt an erection starting.

"Sulking or not, I'm here now. Now what are you going to do with me?"

"Huh?"

"See, you have no idea. That's why I need to be in charge."

"I'm used to being the one in charge...not that anything's going to happen. Believe me, it's not."

Tamara downed her drink and signaled the bartender. He returned with her drink and two more shots of tequila. She pushed one toward him and arched her eyebrow. Nate returned her gaze and held it for a moment before reluctantly picking up the glass. They clinked and tossed back the shots. He had to admit that this one went down a lot easier and he was starting to relax. When he put the shot glass down he made sure he had the bartender's attention and waved his hand over the top of it. He certainly didn't need any more.

Tamara licked her lips again. "You only think you want to be in charge, most men think they're supposed to be. That's just a relic from the caveman days."

"You're wrong."

"Am I? I'm pretty good at reading people, that's why I've done well in sales. You'll be much happier if you don't go against your true nature."

"It is my true nature, as you call it."

"You sure about that?"

Nate was insistent but deep down he wondered if she might be right. He quickly reflected on some of the hottest times he'd had with Cynthia. The ones that stood out – and most turned him on – were the times she took the initiative starting with the incident on New Year's Eve. Still, he remembered plenty of times, most of them actually, where he took the leadership role. No, he was sure it was the variety he liked.

"I'm sure."

"I'm going to ask you a question and I want an honest answer...the first thing that comes to mind."

"Okay"

"Look at me. I mean take a really, really good look."

Tamara stood up and moved the stool out of the way. She stood with her hands held out, palm up and very slowly turned around until she had done a complete three-sixty. He looked at her gorgeous face, great boobs, magnificent ass and, when she turned back around, her crotch where he could just make out the fold of her pussy lips through the tight jeans. She sat back down and looked at him.

"Okay," she said. "I want an honest answer, lightning quick: if you could do one, and only one, sexual act with me what would it be?"

Nate didn't hesitate. "Eat your pussy."

Tamara laughed. "Not fuck me, or have me blow you? Or have me do anything to you at all? No, you want to eat *me*. Doesn't sound like someone in charge, more like someone who wants to serve me."

"I looked at you and thought it would be tasty."

"It is, believe me it is."

Nate was a little unnerved. They just met yet she seemed to totally have the upper hand. What if she was right? Did it really matter? So what if he wanted to eat her, he'd fuck her afterward. The bartender put down another tequila and he downed it without hesitation. Did she know him better than he knew himself?

Tamara drank her shot. "It's nothing to be ashamed of. You have to be the strong one when you're out in the world, most guys do. Private time is your chance to be yourself. Plenty of guys like it when a woman takes charge; some like to be tied up, bossed around, spanked and it's okay."

Nate realized he had a massive erection. He was watching her profile as she looked toward the bartender. He eyed her boobs and wondered what her nipples were like. He imagined Tamara tying him up and spanking him. It wasn't unpleasant....not unpleasant at all.

# Chapter Ten

The Rabbit Hole wasn't very busy when Cynthia got there. Friday had a lot of business people celebrating the end of the workweek by enjoying happy hour, Saturday was more sedate. She chose a stool near the middle of the bar intending to have a cocktail before sitting down for dinner. She wasn't one to go out alone, especially to a bar, but right now it was what she needed. She gave the bartender her order as watched as he prepared her drink. A few moments later he set a perfectly crafted raspberry martini down in front of her. A big sip resulted in a satisfied smile.

Cynthia finished her drink and decided to have one more before eating dinner. She was in no rush at all and was having a nice time just sitting there and watching the people. One guy, much younger than her, approached her but she made it clear she wasn't interested. It did make her feel good though. The place had filled up a bit and there were only a few seats left at the bar. One woman came in, asked her if the stool next to her was taken and sat down when Cynthia assured her it wasn't. She was probably in her mid-forties, with blonde hair from a bottle, boobs from a surgeon, and an ass from too much chocolate. Her face looked a bit tired and she wore a little too much makeup trying to conceal the inevitable advancement of age. Cynthia glanced at the woman's hand and saw there was no wedding band. Her immediate impression was one of a divorced woman desperately trying to find love as her looks and youth deserted her. It was exactly what she was afraid of becoming.

The woman turned to her. "Hi, I'm Samantha – Sam."

"Cynthia." She shook the woman's hand.

Sam glanced Cynthia's ring. "Waiting for your husband?"

"No, he's away on business. I felt like getting out for a drink. You? Waiting for someone?"

"You could say that. I'm hoping to meet someone one of these days."

"*In here?*"

Cynthia regretted that as soon as she said it. Her tone made it come out all wrong and Sam's expression changed. She realized she'd touched a nerve. She took a sip of her martini and hoped she could make it right.

"I didn't mean," Cynthia said. "I just..."

"It's okay. I must seem like a desperate old hag searching for love in a meat market."

"No, of course not."

Samantha took a gulp from her vodka and tonic. "You're what, thirty three, thirty-five?"

"Almost forty?"

"No way...really? Damn you look good."

"Thanks."

Samantha rummaged through her purse and pulled out what Cynthia thought was a cigarette. She was about to tell her there was no smoking in here when she realized in was one of those nicotine vaporizers. She finished her martini and motioned to the bartender for one more, dinner would have to wait just a little longer.

Sam blew out a wisp of vapor. "I was forty-four when my husband dumped me for a younger model. Five years later I'm still trying to find someone."

"I'm sorry," Cynthia said.

"Don't be. Karma's a bitch and it got him good. His sweet young thing dumped him but not before cleaning him out."

"Have you been meeting anyone at all?"

"Oh sure, I get dates. Too often I find out they're married, liars, or jerks....usually all three."

Cynthia laughed. "They can't all be that bad."

Samantha shook her head. "No and I have met some decent guys, even had a couple longer term relationships that just didn't work out."

"You'll find someone."

"I try to keep my sense of humor and have fun. Hey, at least I can still get laid."

There it was again. Getting laid. Intercourse. Sex. Cynthia wondered if she'd ever have it again. Real sex, the kind she enjoyed so much not that long ago. Making love. With a man she loved and who loved her. She was starting to feel sorry for herself when Samantha started laughing, almost losing control.

"What's so funny?" Cynthia asked.

"I was just thinking of the last guy I had sex with," Sam said. "Or tried to anyway."

"What happened?"

"I was drunk and horny as hell...and home alone. I went online looking for a hookup and saw this guy I'd chatted with a few times but never met. He told me how good he was – they all say that –and bragged about his eight-inch cock. I figured what the hell."

"Just like that?"

"Like I said, I was drunk. I went to his apartment and to my surprise he actually looked like his picture. He undressed me and he really wasn't bad....ate me pretty good. Then I undid his pants and dropped his shorts and that's when it happened."

"What?"

"I couldn't help it, I just started laughing. He was erect, he was proud, and he was barely five inches. I said 'where's the rest of it?' and laughed so hard I was crying."

"Oh my god, you didn't."

"I did. He got so pissed that he threw me out, pushed me right out the door naked. He tossed my clothes after me and I had to get dressed in the hallway."

Cynthia had tears in her eyes. "That is just too funny."

Samantha laughed along with her. "Guys have so much ego invested in their dicks, too bad half of them don't know how to measure them let alone use them."

They chatted a bit longer until Samantha decided it was time to go because there were no guys worth hanging around for. She was going to try her luck at another bar and invited Cynthia to come along but she declined. Instead she finished her martini and went to the dining room. After three drinks she was feeling the liquor and knew she had to eat something substantial. She sat alone at a table that gave her a good view of the place so she could people-watch while she had dinner. A salad, Chicken Piccata, and even a piece of cheesecake for desert did the trick. She paid the bill, left a generous tip and got up to head home. The night had been exactly what she hoped for.

Cynthia decided to use the bathroom before leaving. After taking care of business she washed up at the sink and studied her reflection in the mirror. She was pleased with what she saw and made herself a vow that regardless of what happens she would never allow herself to look as tired and worn out as Samantha. She left the restroom and walked past the bar on her way to the exit. Her heart skipped a beat when she spotted Zach sitting at a corner stool. She made a sharp right turn and sat down at the same stool she had at been before. Time for one more raspberry martini before going home.

# Chapter Eleven

Nate and Tamara had moved to the end of the bar where they had more privacy. He was feeling the alcohol and assumed she was too. He had a beer in front of him but he was drinking it in slow motion as he looked at the earrings dangling from her lobes – even her ears were perfect. He wished she'd worn the low-cut top she had on the day before but at the same time was glad she hadn't because it was already difficult enough not to stare. He gave up trying to move the conversation away from sex.

"It's not that different from sales," Tamara said. "You figure out the needs first, then the wants."

"Aren't they all 'wants'?"

"No, some things are the needs for basic survival, food and shelter for example. Wants are the nice house, fancy car, summer cabin on the lake."

"So how does this tie in to sex?" he asked.

"The need to procreate is a basic need. Getting horny is your body's way of saying 'go make babies' so the species survives. The animal instinct says the male should be the aggressor but Freud will tell you that societal pressure creates different needs which translate into fetishes."

"Maybe it's the booze, but I don't quite follow."

"Then we need more booze."

Tamara waved the bartender down and two more tequila shots appeared. He stopped trying to protest and accepted the fact that he was going to get drunk and he was well on his way. He respected Tamara's ability to hold her liquor, she had just as much as he did but he couldn't detect any sign that she wasn't in total control. The tequila arrived, they saluted each other with the glasses and drank them down.

Tamara wiped her lips with her fingers. "Let me try again. Society tells people how they're 'supposed' to act. That may go against what they really feel so they develop cravings, or fetishes."

"Like being dominated?"

"Yes, though that's not really a fetish, just a power preference."

"Power preference?"

"Yes, whether you prefer to be passive or assertive."

"Like you needing to be in charge."

"Exactly, that's how I enjoy it. If you were to tie me up and put me in a passive position I wouldn't enjoy that, other people love it."

Nate laughed. "I guess I can put away the rope."

"Nah, I'll use it on you. Understand it doesn't mean I won't do what you want, I just do it on my terms. I'll give you a killer blowjob but I'll suck your cock when I want."

"What if I don't want you to suck it?"

"There you go again, forgetting who's in charge."

Nate's erection was back as he pictured Tamara giving him that "killer blowjob." He was watching her tongue as she talked and could almost feel it working on his cock. This woman wasn't like any he had met before, she was so uninhibited. While he wondered what sex with her would be like, he wasn't sure he could measure up to her obviously high standards. Not that he would find out anytime soon. She was saying something but he didn't catch it.

"I was saying were you passive or aggressive the last time you fucked?"

"I don't remember, it was so long ago."

He regretted the statement before the words were out of his mouth. The tequila had loosened his tongue and now he would have to explain even though it wasn't really any of her business.

"You're married," she said. "Don't you guys fuck?"

"Not anymore."

Tamara's eyes widened a bit. "How long has it been?"

Nate thought for a moment. "Probably six months since I last put my dick in her cunt."

"Ooh, I sense a bit of hostility," she said. "Was it always like that?"

The can of worms had been opened so he told her the entire story. As the words came out it made him sad to think of the way it used to be compared to now. When they used to fuck. When Cynthia *liked* to fuck. He was beginning to think it would never be the same again.

"I hate to say it but there's no way your marriage will survive if you don't fix it."

"She doesn't seem to want to."

"Bullshit. The woman you described is not going to go without sex forever. If you don't fuck her she'll end up with someone who will – if she hasn't already."

"She wouldn't do that."

"You sure about that?"

Nate thought for a moment. How could he be sure? He didn't see any signs of an affair, she was just a woman who lost interest. But if the fire returned would it be with him, or would someone else reignite the spark? How could he really know?

"Two things I know for sure," Tamara said.

"What?"

"You need to face the fact that you are passive and learn to enjoy it..."

"And?"

"You need to get laid."

Tamara stood up, threw some cash on the bar and grabbed her purse. He made no effort to get up. She came over, put an arm around him and squeezed. Then she gave him a soft and quick kiss on the lips.

She looked at him intently. "Room three-sixteen, in one hour."

"No, I don't think..."

She started walking away. "You'll be there."

# Chapter Twelve

Despite the food Cynthia was still feeling her three drinks and now she was a good way through her fourth. She wasn't sure why she ordered it, she could have just as easily had coffee. It was a spontaneous decision when she eyed Zach sitting at the bar. She had no desire to be picked up and certainly had no intention of encouraging him. She just liked the attention he gave her the night before and wanted a little again. He made her feel like a desirable woman for the first time in a long time. The only problem was he didn't seem to recognize her even though he had looked her way. Maybe he did know who she was and just wasn't interested. Perhaps, she hoped, he was just being respectful after what she told him last night.

Cynthia took a good look at herself in the bar mirror. She did look good tonight, certainly better than last night. She leaned forward a little and discretely squeezed her arms together causing a good deal of cleavage to show. Whatever Zach might think she was looking at a desirable woman and she hadn't thought about herself that way in a very long time. To her this meant that the night was a rousing success. Now if she could only get Nate to see her this way again. She drained the last of her martini and put the glass down and pushed it across the bar along with a five dollar bill as a tip. Just as she was swiveling her chair to get up the bartender placed a fresh raspberry martini in front of her.

"Oh, I didn't want another."

The bartender nodded toward the end of the bar. "It's from the gentleman over there. He says it's good to see an old friend again."

Surprised, but feeling good, she turned back into the bar, lifted her glass and raised it toward Zach in thanks. She figured she would wait for him to come over, have a few sips and then tell him she had to leave. By the time she was half-way done he still hadn't come over even though he had glanced at her and smiled a few times. He continued talking to the older man next to him. She certainly wasn't going to go over to him. She would take another sip and then say goodbye to him as she was leaving. A few minutes later she was almost to the end of the drink when he got up and started in her direction. She gathered her purse so she could be standing when he got there. She was about to rise when she felt the buzz of the booze and thought she better wait a minute.

Zach reached her chair. "I was hoping I would see you again sometime but I never thought it would be so soon. How are you?"

"Fine, but I..."

"I know, you're married. Cynthia, right?"

"Yes"

"Good, I didn't want to mess that up. I'm..."

"Zach"

He smiled. "You remembered. I'm flattered."

Cynthia was feeling a bit flustered, a combination of booze, nervousness and sexual excitement. Zach nodded to the bartender and another martini appeared. She was already well on her way to getting trashed, she couldn't possibly have another. She started to protest but Zach held up his hand as if to say she didn't have to drink it.

"I thought you might want another as you waited for your friend."

"She already left," Cynthia lied.

"Oh, I didn't realize you'd been here a while."

"I just had some dinner and was about to head home."

Zach looked disappointed. "Well, I won't keep you. But I'd love it if you stayed and chatted a minute or two."

"Maybe a couple of minutes."

"Fantastic! I don't want to sound forward, I know you're married, but you looked great last night but tonight you are absolutely gorgeous."

Cynthia felt herself blush. *Gorgeous?* She couldn't recall the last time any man had said that to her let alone a guy who looked like Zach. She nervously took a gulp of her martini. Her mind was a blur as Zach was telling her about himself and asking her questions about what she had for dinner, movies she liked, books she read. The minutes passed quickly, she emptied her drink and another one appeared. She was no longer on her way to getting trashed, she was downright hammered. And she didn't care. She noticed Zach's eyes on her boobs, only glancing at first but now he was locked on to her cleavage. She didn't care about that either. She looked at him and smiled waiting for him to look up. When he finally did he realized he'd been caught and this time he was the one blushing.

Zach quickly recovered. "That's...that's an interesting pendant."

She fingered the chain and suspended the pendant in such a way that when he looked at it he had to look right down her blouse. As he watched him her nipples became fully erect. As they tried to break free of her bra Zach's eyes went wide.

"Thank you, I've had it for years. It's my favorite piece of jewelry."

"You wear it well," he said.

"It fits in there perfectly, no?" *Cynthia, what are you saying. God I'm drunk.*

That was it she knew she had to go. She stood up and immediately felt dizzy and grabbed the back of the stool for support. He saw her wobble and his very strong hand grabbed her arm above the elbow to steady her. She would have to call a cab, she probably couldn't find her car let alone drive it. She fumbled through her purse looking for her phone but couldn't locate it and gave up.

Zach stood up. "I think we better get you outside for some air."

"Good...that's a....that's a very good idea."

Cynthia took her purse and slung the strap over her shoulder. She started walking but lurched back to the bar, took her drink and downed the remnants in one gulp. With both arms cling to Zach's very big bicep she staggered toward the door. The cool night air hit her as they walked outside and she felt a little less inebriated. They were walking along the street but in the opposite direction of her car.

"I think...I think I better call a cab."

"We'll do that in a few minutes, let's sober you up a little first then we'll get you home."

"You're so sweet, thank you."

Zach put his arm around her shoulder and pulled her close. Cynthia squeezed him back and realized how good it felt to hold someone again even if she was drunk. She looked up at him and he stopped, bent toward her and kissed her softly on the lips. Her mouth opened and she felt his tongue explore hers. A few seconds later, short of breath, she pulled away.

"I'm sorry...I can't."

Zach put his finger on her lips. "It's okay, I understand. Kissing a beautiful woman made my night."

They resumed walking and things began to get even hazier for Cynthia. She felt like they walked forever and she was just trying to stay upright. Several times she felt like she was about to pass out. She couldn't keep track of the turns or how far they walked. They reached a building and Zach led her inside. She didn't recognize it but there was some sort of lobby where she sat for few minutes before he led her down a hallway and stopped in front of an elevator. The door opened and they got on.

"Where...where are we going?"

"Someplace safe."

# Chapter Thirteen

Nate left the bar about thirty minutes or so after Tamara departed. The street was fairly empty during the walk back to the hotel, it was, after all, well past midnight. The night air revived him a bit and his head started to clear. He was not used to doing shots, let alone shots of tequila. By his count he did four, or was it five shots? Add half a dozen pints of beer to that and it was little wonder he had quite a buzz. He tried to remember how the line went – *one tequila, two tequila, three tequila, floor!*

The desk clerk nodded to him as he walked into the hotel. He went to the bar and looked in, no sign of Marc or anyone else he cared to talk to. He thought about having a coffee but figured it wouldn't be a good idea before bed, instead he purchased a bottle of water at the hotel convenience shop. Nate took a healthy swig then headed for the elevator. The door opened immediately, he got on and pushed "eight" and the doors closed. He got out on his floor, walked the few steps to the hallway and turned right. He stopped almost immediately, paused for a moment, turned around and went back to the elevator pushing the down button. Again, the door opened right away and he stepped in. His finger hovered for a moment then pushed "three" and the doors closed. He got off on the third floor, made a right at the hallway and walked to room three-sixteen. He was about to knock when the door opened and Tamara let him in.

She looked at her watch. "Right on time."

"I'm not staying, I just wanted to talk to you for a minute."

"Make yourself comfortable, I'll be right back."

Tamara went to her bathroom and closed the door. He heard the shower running so he sat down in the armchair next to the sofa. Her room was much nicer than his with a separate sitting area in an alcove. He tossed his empty water bottle in her trash and opened her mini-bar refrigerator to get another one. Instead he selected a beer and sat back down to wait. The shower stopped and he head her moving around. A few minutes later she came out where a dark blue, very short, silk robe. Her hair was tied back and her makeup gone – she still looked gorgeous. Her now unfettered breasts strained against the fabric of the tightly-tied robe. Even without the bra they were firm and he could just make out the tips of her nipples.

She sat on the sofa and curled her bare legs under her in a way that the bottom of her right butt cheek was slightly exposed.

Tamara saw that Nate had a beer and went to the min-bar to get one herself. She reached for it and her robe slid up revealing just a sliver of her bare bottom. Nate felt his erection grow as she sat back down and curled her feet up again. She reached her beer across the small gap between them and the clinked bottles before she took a drink. She just looked at him without saying anything as if she was appraising him. It made Nate feel a bit vulnerable and uncomfortable so he took a big gulp from his bottle.

"So Nate, what is it you wanted to talk about?"

He took a sip of beer. "I was thinking about what you said...about embracing my passive side. I'm not exactly sure how. Am I supposed to just lay there and do nothing?"

Tamara laughed. "No, that's not what I mean at all. Keep doing what you've always done, just allow yourself to be led as well."

"How so?"

"Follow your partner's lead. If the woman is like me and totally dominant just do what she says. Most aren't that way. What you need to do is pay attention to her cues and take them wherever they may go."

"Cues I can follow, I like to think I do that now. I don't know that I could be totally dominated though."

"Sure you could."

"I don't think so."

Tamara put her bottle on the table. "Let's try an experiment. Stand in front of me here."

He hesitated then put his bottle down and stood up. He came around a stood in front of her, about five feet away. She sat there looking at him, her eyes moving up and down. He began to feel a little uncomfortable again, as if he were under a microscope, a feeling that was magnified by the buzz from the alcohol.

Tamara stood. "You'll need to remove your shirt....go ahead, just take it off."

Nate pulled his shirt over his head and tossed it on the bed as she sat back down. She eyed him again with the tip of her tongue seductively touching her upper lip. He grew hard and it had to be obvious to her.

"Now just stand there and look straight ahead with your hands at your side."

She stood up again, as she did so her robe billowed open and he caught an eyeful of both breasts including the nipples. She walk around him slowly. Her hand brushed against the muscles of his shoulder and continued around to his pectorals as she walked. Difficult as it was, his hands remained at his side but he had trouble looking in front of him.

"Keep looking straight ahead no matter what, hands at your side."

Nate did so as she came around in front of him almost touching. With her face no more than two inches from his she looked directly into his eyes. Her hands reached his belt and opened it. Her eyes never left his. She undid the button and lowered the zipper, eyes never wavering. In one motion she backed away and yanked his pants and underwear down to the level of his knees. His cock was sticking straight out and he was so shocked he almost came on the spot but that moment quickly passed but his erection was harder than it had been in a very long time. She dropped back onto the sofa.

"Stay there exactly like that, hands at your side. Don't you dare move no matter what. Do you understand me?"

"Yes"

"Good"

Tamara looked at him for a moment then untied her robe. She slipped the arms out, lifted her ass, pulled the robe off and tossed it aside. The word that came to mind was "exquisite." Her breasts were large, perfectly round, obviously natural with beautiful, oval nipples. Though partially shaved, she had a thick strip of pubic hair and pussy lips that weren't too large. Everything about her was perfect. He had a difficult time just standing there but he managed to do so. He almost lost it when she put one leg up and spread it wide. The fingers of her right hand gently spread the lips and she slowly stroked herself while her left hand gently massaged her left breast and squeezed her erect nipple. She bit her lower lip and let out a soft moan as she rubbed her clit. Her eyes never left his.

"You're doing good. Don't move."

She was putting on quite a show for him and Nate had a urge to grab his cock and stroke it as he watched her masturbate. She worked her clit, inserted fingers in her vagina, massaged her boobs. She started squirming and breathing fast and shallow and he waited for her orgasm. She suddenly stopped, slid around and planted both feet on the floor in front of her.

"Eat me now!"

He dropped to his knees directly in front of her and lowered his face to her pussy. He worked his tongue up the labia and to her clit. She let out a gasp and both her hands grabbed his hair, clenched it with her fingers and pulled him in tight. It hurt like hell but he didn't care. Her thighs started to quiver as she pulled him in so hard he couldn't breathe. She arched her back, shoving her pussy hard into his face as she shuddered.

"*Arrgghhh! Yes! Yes!*"

Nate pulled away and gasped for air. She was right, it was absolutely delicious.

Tamara stood up. "On the bed now!

Nate kicked off the pants that were wrapped around his ankles and went to the bed. She was sitting upright waiting for him. He climbed in and she nudged him on his back. Straddling his waist, she reached for his cock and hovered over him. She slowly lowered herself on his penis and he thought he might cum. The length of time since he was last inside a woman made him extremely sensitive and he didn't think he would last long at all. She lowered herself until he was all the way in sitting on him with her palms on his chest and paused for a moment.

Tamara looked him in the eye. "Don't you dare cum until I tell you."

Nate closed his eyes as she started to move up and down. He tried to focus on something other than his cock. He was right on the edge and barely managing to hold it. He opened his eyes and watched her. Her face was contorted in pleasure, her eyes closed and she lightly bit her lip. He reached his hands up to cup her breasts. They were amazingly soft, full, and heavier than he expected. She moaned and picked up speed, moving up with each motion to the point she was almost off him and them slamming herself back down. He couldn't hold it any longer and he ejaculated.

"*Arrgghh!*"

Tamara didn't stop until she came loudly herself and settled down on him and catching her breath. She pushed herself back up with him still inside her.

"I didn't say you could come...now eat your cream pie!"

She climbed up an straddled his face. He saw his semen dripping out of her as she brought her pussy to his mouth. He licked away his cum and tasted its saltiness. She rocked back and forth as he licked her. When he reached her clit she shuddered lightly and let out a low gasp as she came again. She got off him, out of the bed and went into the bathroom. He lay back and relaxed himself. A minute or two later he heard the bathroom door open.

"Come in here."

Nate got up and went to her. She was still naked and sitting on the closed toilet lid. She motioned for him to come over to her and when he did she pulled him close. She fondled his balls and stroked his cock. He started coming back to life. When he was semi-erect she took him in her mouth and worked him slowly. She was incredible and he was fully hard in no time at all. When she was satisfied that he was at maximum altitude and not in danger of deflating she pushed him back and stood up. While holding his cock and stroking it, she moved a couple of steps over to the sink facing the mirror. she bent over watching his reflection and spread her legs apart.

With her intently watching he inserted himself into her very wet pussy.

"This time you can cum whenever you want."

With his hands on her hips he began to thrust slowly. He was much more in control this time and enjoyed the feeling of every stroke and thrust. She was enjoying it too as she rocked back into him. It was several minutes before he felt his orgasm starting. When it was almost there he leaned over onto her, her back supporting his weight. He cupped her breasts in both hands and let out a grunt as he came. She turned around and, for the first time, kissed him deeply. She pulled away, looked at him and smiled.

"How was that? You were totally passive through it all."

"Absolutely and unbelievably amazing. I haven't enjoyed it that much in a long, long time."

"Told you so," she said. "Just one more thing to do. Get in the tub...go on, get in."

Nate was puzzled but he did as she said. It was slightly oversize so he fit well. She had him slide down with his head resting against the rim and his arms lengthwise along the edge. When he was settled she stepped in shimmied up toward his head, placed her knees on the side in a way that pinned his arms. She brought her crotch to his face and he reached his tongue out to meet her pussy. Just before they touched she stopped. She took a deep breath, gritted her teeth and began to urinate forcefully. The hot, salty golden torrent landed on his tongue and in his mouth before he could close it. She continued to piss a steady stream all over his face and chest. He was pinned in such a way that he was helpless until she finally stopped. When she was done she shoved her pussy forward and waited for him to lick it clean. When it was clear that she wasn't going to move he reluctantly tongued the last of the salty droplets off of her. When she was satisfied he was done she got up and looked down at him in the tub.

"That was for cumming before I said it was okay."

# Chapter Fourteen

Sunlight streamed across Cynthia's face, her lids fluttered and eyes opened. Searing pain coursed through her brain, her temples throbbed. Her head still on the pillow, she looked about at the strange surroundings. Alarmed, she sat up and tried to take stock. A wave of nausea ran through her and she started to retch. Taking a deep breath she put her head back down and closed her eyes. When the nausea passed she sat up again very slowly and looked around. Her clothes were strewn about the room and she realized that she was totally naked.

The utilitarian furniture, pastoral reproductions hanging on the wall, writing desk and corner chair told her she was in a hotel room. She moved gingerly and looked at herself. Her vagina was sore, she reached her finger down and wiped the moisture from her pussy, brought it to her mouth and tasted it. Semen. She also saw dried semen on her thigh. With her head pounding, she slowly gathered up her clothes as she looked for her purse. Her body was sore all over and she was fighting the urge to throw up so she dropped to her knees and crawled around the room as she searched. She reached the chair and saw the purse under her pink panties. As she sat on the floor, her back against the chair, it started coming back to her and she closed her eyes.

They were walking down the street when he put his arm around her and then he kissed her and she felt the electricity. The feeling of human contact had been missing for so long. She protested but wanted it, really wanted it. They walked again and came to the hotel and went inside. She sat in the lobby while he went to the reception desk, then they went up the elevator and to the room. She knew what she was doing was wrong, very wrong but she needed it so bad. The door closed behind them and he spun her around and they kissed for what seemed like an eternity. His hands brushed her nipples through her clothes and she shuddered. He deftly unfastened her buttons while their tongues explored each other. He slipped off her blouse as he bent down to kiss her breasts. He reached behind and unfastened the clasp of her bra and slipped it off allowing her boobs to hang free.
"Oh my God, they're beautiful!"

He sucked gently on each nipple and led her to the bed and sat her down on the edge. While he unbuttoned his shirt she undid his belt and lowered the zipper. As he slipped his shirt off she lowered his trousers to the floor and he stepped out of them. She ran her hand across the bulge in his underwear. Pulling down his briefs revealed that he was large with a nice mushroom head and, thankfully, circumcised. She stroked him as she looked up at him and smiled. She looked at his cock for a second before taking it in her mouth as far as she could and then moving back up slowly as she applied pressure to the bottom of the shaft with her tongue.

"Oh, that's nice."

She continued, varying the tongue action and pressure, starting, stopping and starting again. She could tell he was about to explode when he stopped her. As she pulled back she saw a drop of cum on the tip. He pushed her back on the bed, unfastened her jeans and pulled them off. He ran his hands lightly up the inside of her thighs causing her to shiver. His fingers found the elastic band of her panties and he slowly lowered them, his eyes fixed on her now very wet pussy.

"I'm sorry I don't shave."

"That's because you're a woman, not a young girl," he said. "Real women don't shave."

He kissed and licked the inside of her thighs and worked his way up at an agonizingly slow pace. He kissed around her pubic triangle, kissed her hair and then, finally, her pussy lips. His tongue parted them and entered her vagina, probing and licking. Her hand found the back of his head and she pulled him higher until his tongue found her clit.

"*Aggghhhhh! Oh yes, yes!*"

She had one orgasm after another, each more powerful than the last. She had both hands on his head as she squirmed with delight. She reached a point where she almost couldn't take it anymore when he stopped. He pulled her up and they switched places with him on his back. She straddled him and took his cock in her hand and guided it as she slowly lowered herself onto him. Her hands were on his muscular pectorals as she steadied herself and moved up and down, going faster with each repetition. Her body convulsed as she came again as he started to moan. In one motion he flipped her on her back, his cock still in her, and started pumping furiously and shoved himself as deep as he could, cried out and came. He went still and they held each other tight.

She felt his penis go soft as it slipped out of her. She purred softly as he pulled away a little. He didn't get up, instead he nudged her and had her lay on her stomach. Her head was on the pillow, her hands under it. He kissed the back of her neck and worked his way down her back until he reached her ass. He massaged and kissed each cheek for several minutes. He took one of the pillows and slid it under her to prop her ass up. He spread her legs apart and surprised her when his tongue found her clit from behind.

"*Oh God!*"

The angle created by this position was an entirely new sensation for her and she came again. His tongue licked her lips and then her anus. No one had ever done that before *and she liked it.* He pushed the tip of his tongue inside her ass and spent a lot of time there and she realized that he wanted to fuck her up the ass. Being very drunk, this excited her but she was scared because he was so large and it would hurt a lot. Just as she made up her mind that she would let him do it he stopped and turned her on her back. He straddled her chest and started rubbing his erect cock between her boobs. She used her hands to squeeze them together as he moved back and forth. His head was leaning back as he thrust, his eyes closed and obviously ready to cum. He got off of her and sat back against the head board and tugged her to him. She went between his legs and took her in her mouth just as he ejaculated. She took him as deep as she could and felt his hot cum and tasted the saltiness and savored every drop as she swallowed it all. They held each other and fell asleep.

Cynthia opened her eyes, her temples still pounding. She climbed on the chair and sat back. She opened and closed her eyes several times as the magnitude of the night before hit her head on.

*"What have I done? What the fuck have I done?"*

She rifled through her bag. Her wallet was still there and appeared to be intact. She found her cell phone and hoped it was still charged. She hit the button and was relieved to see the battery at fifty percent. The screen showed she had missed seven calls, one from Nate the other six from Kelly. She listened to the voicemail. Message from Kelly asking her to call. Message from Kelly again. Nate wishing her goodnight and confirming his pickup time tomorrow. *Shit, that's today.* Message from Kelly again sounding concerned. Message from a now frantic Kelly. Before she could listen to the next one the phone vibrated. She looked at the caller ID – Kelly.

"Hello"

"Where the fuck are you? I've been going crazy."

"I...I don't know."

"What? What don't you know?"

Cynthia started to sob. "I...I don't know where I am."

"What? Calm down. What do you mean you don't know where you are?"

"Oh Kelly, I fucked up...I fucked up so bad."

"Easy girl. Deep breath, let's figure out where you are."

"I'm in some sort of hotel room."

"Hotel? If it's a hotel it should say something ....look for the phone. What does it say?"

She scanned the room and saw the phone on the writing desk. She went to it and looked for the hotel name.

"Got it. I'm at the Holbrook Hotel."

"That's all the way across town. Are you safe?"

"Yes, I'm safe."

"Okay, I'm coming to get you. I have to drop the kids at my neighbor so it'll take me at least twenty minutes. What room are you in."

"I don't know."

"Look at the phone. it should say."

"Six-thirteen.....room six-thirteen."

"I'm on my way, sit tight."


Still naked, Cynthia gathered her clothes and jumped in the shower for a quick rinse. She felt the soreness of her vagina as she washed it. Her nipples were tender from being bitten. She ran the soap up the crack of her butt cheeks and remembered how good it felt when he licked her anus. She was majorly hung over and it showed when she looked in the mirror. At least she didn't feel like she was going to throw up any longer. She toweled off and dressed herself. She went back to the chair, sat down and closed her eyes.

Cynthia was startled by a tap on the door. She looked through the peephole, saw Kelly and opened the door. Her friend walked in and gave her a huge hug as her eyes scanned the room taking in the unmade bed. Kelly pushed away, still holding her arms and looked at her.

"You look like hell. What happened?"

Cynthia wiped at a tear that fell down her cheek. "Oh Kelly, don't judge me, please don't judge me...please."

Kelly's mouth fell open. "When have I *ever* judged you? Now tell me everything."

# Chapter Fifteen

TSA checkpoint lines were long, typical of a Sunday at Kansas City International Airport. Nate was several hours early because he wanted to get out of the hotel and he would meet Marc for lunch and a few beers, though he might pass on the beers after the night before. The company meeting was short that morning since many of the attendees, including Tamara, needed to catch early flights home. As the line snaked slowly toward the metal detectors Nate glanced at his watch, Tamara would be almost halfway home by now.

Morning had come quickly since Nate didn't get back to his room until almost three. It seemed as if his head just hit the pillow when the phone rang with his wakeup call. He sleepwalked his way through his morning routine as he thought about the night before. Tamara had been absolutely amazing. Only one previous lover could match her in his mind – Cynthia. Strangely, he felt no guilt and wasn't sure what that meant. One thing became crystal clear to him, though he loved his wife he was not going to go through the remainder of his life without an active sex life. He didn't want a divorce by any stretch of the imagination but the status quo was totally unacceptable.

At the security checkpoint he placed his carry-on on the conveyor, emptied his pockets, took of his shoes and belt and walked through the metal detector. He waited while his bag was screened then reassembled himself. On the other side he walked toward his gate and spotted the bar he would be meeting Marc at. His friend was already there and as he approached he saw a beer waiting for him, so much for not drinking. He dropped his bag and sat on the stool as he shook Marc's hand.

"Glad that's over with," Marc said.

"I hear you. How'd the ass kissing go?"

"I've got chapped lips. You're lucky, the only ass you have to kiss is mine; I've got half a dozen VPs to deal with."

The first sip of beer was a tentative one. By the time it was half gone Nate was feeling a little more like himself. The after affects of the tequila wasn't as bad as he feared and the "hair of the dog" had him feeling almost normal again. When the beer was gone there was no hesitation in getting a refill. Marc and Nate ordered a couple of hamburgers knowing that there would be no food on their flights and they'd be lucky to get a mini bag of stale pretzels. They chatted about the conference while they ate and when they finished there was time for one more beer before boarding. Nate was thankful that Tamara hadn't come up in conversation but his luck didn't hold.

"So how was last night?"

"Okay, had a few beers at the *Sly Fox* with a group from the company."

"Was Tamara there?"

"She was."

"I've never had a chance to hang with her socially. I bet she's fun."

"That's she is, she's quite an interesting character."

"I hear she's a real pisser."

"You have no idea."

Nate didn't bite on any more of Marc's attempts to talk about Tamara and the subject was finally dropped. The conversation switched to Marc's kids and the various things they were doing. They talked about the next sales conference a year from now and what they would do since it would finally be held in Las Vegas instead of some suburb in the Midwest. It was almost time to leave when Marc asked Nate a serious question.

"What are you going to do about Cynthia? This can't go on forever."

"I know, believe me I know. I just wish I had an inkling that she actually cared and *wanted* to do something about it."

"I can't believe she doesn't, I mean it just doesn't compute. How does a woman go from being a borderline nymphomaniac to a candidate for a nunnery?"

"I wish I had an answer."

"Well I hope you find one soon. A couple like you splitting up would be a real tragedy."

Nate boarded the plane and found his seat. He was next to a young couple who didn't show any interest in him. That meant a peaceful flight without having to have an inane conversation with a total stranger. After the passengers were settled in and the plane's door closed, the flight attendant went over the safety instructions. She reminded everyone to shut off their cell phones and he remembered he hadn't turned his off. He took it out of his pocket and was about to shut it down. Before he did he took one last look at the text from earlier that morning.

> u were awesome,
> im still tingling -
> i owe u a huge 'killer bj'
> – Tamara

# Chapter Sixteen

The waitress put the plates on the table and refilled the coffee. Typical of a Sunday morning, the restaurant was crowded and the servers were looking harried. Cynthia started eating her French Toast very slowly lest the nausea return. Kelly was devouring her ham and cheese omelet like she had just been rescued from being stranded on a desert island. During breakfast Cynthia told her everything she could remember, Kelly asked questions and eventually the entire story unfolded. When she was done Cynthia felt as if she had a big scarlet letter on her forehead that proclaimed her to be a whore. Kelly seemed to disagree.

"Look," Kelly said, "something like this was bound to happen, you've been miserable."

"Maybe so, but it doesn't give me the right to cheat."

"You needed to get laid and it sounds to me like you had fun."

"I did – until the martinis wore off."

"It also sounds like this guy knew how to fuck."

"Did he ever."

"And you needed it."

"But not with a stranger. God, I'm such a shit."

Cynthia lowered her eyes and concentrated on her food. Nate was coming home today and she wasn't sure how she would react. Would he be able to tell? Would she be able to hide it? Despite their difficulties she had never been dishonest with him and she certainly never cheated. She didn't think he did either but even if he had it didn't give her the right to.

"I have to pick Nate up at the airport tonight, how can I even look at him?"

Cynthia took a drink of coffee. "Trust me, you'll be fine."

"How can you be so sure?"

"Because I've been there."

"Huh? What do you mean?"

"I...I never told you, but I cheated on Doug."

"What? When?"

"A couple of years ago, when I went through that period of feeling sorry for myself."

"Why didn't you tell me?"

"It didn't last very long, we only did it a couple of times before I broke it off. I realized what I had to lose. Besides he had a tiny dick and wasn't very good. Not like your guy."

"He's not 'my guy,' he was a stranger."

"Whatever. Tell me, did he have a big cock?"

"Huge, just like Nate."

"Figures. You get the big ones and I'm married to the 'minuteman' and have an affair with 'needle dick the bug-fucker' who has no clue about how to please a woman."

Cynthia laughed, probably for the first time all day. They finished their breakfast, the waitress cleared the dishes and left the check. She reached for it but Kelly grabbed it first and gave her a look that said there would be no argument. They got up and left the restaurant. The conversation continued as they walked to the parking lot.

"So tell me," Kelly asked, "What was your favorite part?"

"Wow, all of it."

"No fair, you can only pick one thing."

Cynthia thought for a moment. "When he licked my asshole."

"Like in passing?"

"No, like he was having it for dinner."

"Wow"

"You know, I feel like a total shit now, but last night he made me feel like a woman again."

They reached their cars and hugged goodbye. Cynthia was about to get in her car when she felt something in the pocket of her jeans. She reached in and pulled out a small piece of paper. She unfolded it and read the words: *You were awesome!* Below was a phone number. A smile spread across her face. She crumpled up the paper and went to toss it away, instead she slipped it back in her pocket.

# Chapter Seventeen

The "fasten seatbelt" light came on just before the Boeing 737 began its descent. The landing gear lowered, flaps came down and the aircraft turned slightly to line up with the runway lights. The wheels touched down with a gentle thud and the nose came down and the thrusters reversed slowing the plane. After taxiing for a few minutes it turned unto the gate, stopped and the interior lights came on. Almost in unison the passengers in the aisle seats stood up and retrieved their bags from the overhead bin.

Being a seasoned traveler, Nate realized there was no hurry and remained seated until it was almost his turn to exit. He stood, retrieved his bag and slowly headed down the aisle, listened to the flight crew thank him for flying with them and walked off the plane and onto the jetway and into the terminal. He took a moment to orient himself and proceeded to baggage claim. Nate reached the carousel for his flight and saw a woman in tight jean and a blouse that couldn't conceal a great rack. She was looking up at the "Arrivals" board oblivious to the guys throwing appreciative glances her way as they walked by. Cynthia looked down from the board and spotted Nate and walked over.

Cynthia kissed him lightly. "Have a good trip?"

"Not bad but a bit tiresome."

"You were probably out carousing with Marc the whole time."

"Only once, and again at the airport today. Seems he has a new title – 'corporate ass-kisser'."

Cynthia chuckled. "Just think, that could have been you."

"Not a chance."

"Hungry?" Cynthia asked. "I never made it to the store so there's nothing in the house. We could go for a burger or grab some takeout."

"Not that hungry, I ate before the flight. Let's just head home."

The bag arrived and they went to the car and out of the airport. Nate kept glancing at his wife as she drove. There was a time when his return after being gone for four days would require immediate sex followed by food. He still found her extremely attractive and she certainly had the ability to turn him on, if only she wanted to. Had she really lost it for good?

The encounter with Tamara had been so hot, so intense, why couldn't he be that way with his own wife? One way or another this issue was going to be resolved. He had the following day off and they were going to have a long talk whether she wanted to or not. As the car sped down the highway he remembered to turn his phone back on. After it powered up the text from Tamara was on the screen, he read it again before returning the device to sleep mode.

Nate retrieved his bag from the trunk and carried it into the house and to the bedroom. He took his suit out and hung it up in the closet but left the rest, he'd take care of it in the morning. Cynthia came into the room, stripped off her jeans and headed into the bathroom to get ready for bed. He took the jeans and put them on a hanger. He hung them in the closet but before closing the door he picked up the crumpled piece of paper that had fallen out of the pocket and onto the floor.

# Chapter Eighteen

Nate's return didn't go the way Cynthia hoped. She wanted things to be right again, the way they used to be. She understood she had let him down and he had every right to be angry with her but this had gone on long enough. She had her plan but never had a chance to put it into action. Gone for four days and he didn't even act like he missed her, went to bed without so much as a good night. She thought they could have dinner and talk – actually talk. Cynthia envisioned an evening of conversation followed by sex, real sex, actual fucking, like Zach had fucked her, fucking the way they used to, when he still loved her. Now she sat up in the bed, Nate with his back to her as if she'd done something wrong. She hadn't even masturbated since she fucked Zach.

Cynthia had a very restless night and was up early. She left the room quietly so Nate could sleep. His company was very reasonable insisting that he take the day off after a weekend conference and she saw no need to wake him up yet. Besides, she wanted him well-rested, he may have avoided her the night before but she wasn't going to allow that to happen again. She brewed some coffee and retrieved the morning paper from the porch. Cynthia was going to prepare breakfast when she remembered she never made it to the grocery store. Instead she poured herself a cup of java and sat down the read the news. She was getting herself a second cup when there was a buzzing noise, Nate had left his phone on the counter. She picked it up and saw a new text on the screen, a weather update that he complained about getting every morning. After reading the forecast she hit the delete button and was about to put the phone down when the previous text message caught her eye. Her face turned ashen.

Tears welled in her eyes as she sat back down, her body trembling lightly. Cynthia tried to gather her thoughts as she heard sounds of her husband stirring coming from the bedroom. The toilet flushed and a moment later he was standing in the doorway as the tears streamed down her face.

She looked at him. "Who's Tamara?"

"Funny, I was going to ask you who thought you were so awesome."

# Chapter Nineteen

The non-descript gray office building looked even more ominous on that overcast Tuesday morning. More than a week had passed since Nate and Cynthia discovered each other's infidelity. At first Nate slept in the guest bedroom but the tension was so thick that he decided to check into a hotel for a few days. The time apart allowed them both to reflect on the issues that led to this point and whether they had the desire to work things out or if it was best to call it quits move on with their lives. Nate knew what he wanted, now in this gloomy edifice he would learn if that was Cynthia's desire as well.

The office of David Blanchard, Marriage and Family Counselor, was significantly more cheerful than the building that housed it. Blanchard was highly recommended but Nate wasn't convinced after his experience with the bereavement counselor a couple years prior. To this point there had only been a brief phone conversation and an extensive questionnaire that he filled out. He didn't have to wait long before he was ushered into the counselor's office. Blanchard stood to greet him and motioned for him to be seated. The adjacent chair was already occupied by his wife. As he sat down Cynthia looked at him and smiled sheepishly. She looked like she hadn't slept in days, Nate's chest tightened with anxiety.

The counselor began. "I've had a chance to review your questionnaires and read your statements. All of that is meaningless unless each of you is willing to commit to resolving the issues that have brought us here. So I ask you – are you truly committed to making your marriage work?"

Nate didn't hesitate. "Absolutely"

Cynthia's eyes welled up with tears. "Yes"

Blanchard shuffled some paper on his desk and made a notation. He read a paper then looked back up at them.

"Things changed at the point of Cynthia's miscarriage, correct? Cynthia, can you please tell me what you believe happened that caused the change."

Cynthia gave a chronological and somewhat clinical version of events that seemed rehearsed. Nate and the counselor listened patiently until she finished.

"Those are the facts," Blanchard said. "But what caused the change?"

Cynthia dabbed at her eyes with a tissue. "It was my fault that I lost the baby."

Wide-eyed, Nate turned to her. "What? That's ridiculous."

"When the doctor told me I would never be able to have children....that's when I knew he hated me."

"*What?*"

"He never touched me after that – unless he was drunk."

"That's...that's absurd," Nate said.

"Nate, you have something different to say?"

He took a moment to collect his thoughts. "The bereavement counselor told me Cynthia would need her space and I shouldn't put pressure on her. I waited for her to return to normal but she never did."

"Did you blame her for what happened?" Blanchard asked.

"What? Of course not. I mean I was upset, but I wasn't angry at her. I certainly didn't think it was her fault. This whole thing is my fault."

Cynthia's eyes never left him. "No"

"How is it your fault?" the counselor asked.

"Because I didn't realize how much she was hurting. She didn't need space, she needed me – and I wasn't there for her."

"Oh Nate..."

Cynthia left her chair, sat on Nate's lap and threw her arms around him as she sobbed. Tears rolled down Nate's cheeks as he held her tightly. Blanchard waited patiently for them to unwind from each other and sit in separate chairs again. Their hands reached across the gap between the chairs, their fingers intertwined.

Blanchard smiled at them. "One of my favorite movie lines, from *Cool Hand Luke,* fits this situation: 'What we have here is a failure to communicate'."

For the rest of the time remaining in there session Blanchard gave them tips and techniques for keeping the lines of communication open. He stressed that it wouldn't be easy because their habits developed over a lifetime and it's easy to fall into old patterns and routines. He gave them homework to do and set a follow up session four weeks out. He asked if they had any questions.

Cynthia spoke. "Just one, but it's a big one. How do we get our sex life back?"

"Very carefully," Blanchard said. He handed her a piece of paper. "Here's the name of a licensed sex therapist that I highly recommend. I strongly suggest you call her."

They walked to their cars hand-in-hand. Nate was beyond relieved. It bothered Nate that his wife slept with a stranger but he couldn't be mad at her because she'd done the same. They did it for the same reason – the need for human contact. Had he been there for her neither one of them would have strayed so, in his mind, it was entirely his fault. They reached her car and Nate put his hands on her shoulders and kissed her.

"I'll get my things from the hotel and come home."

Cynthia hesitated. "No, not yet."

"What? Why?"

"Because I don't want to screw this up."

"We won't ..."

"No, listen to me. I want to see the sex therapist first."

"Okay, but..."

"Then I want you to take me on a date."

"A date..."

"Yes, I want to start over."

The expression on her face told him she was dead serious. He was going to do whatever she wanted because he didn't want to screw this up either.

He looked into her eyes. "It's a deal."

"One more thing," she said, "don't think you're getting lucky on the first date – I'm not that kind of girl."

# Chapter Twenty

The building was much more cheerful than the one that housed the marriage counselor. The exterior was a modern glass that reflected the tree-lined surroundings. The entrance had a well-maintained courtyard with benches that allowed visitors and workers alike to sit outside on nice days. The lobby featured paintings and works of modern art that captured the contemporary flavor of the building. Cynthia thought of it as a happy place as she located the office of Glenda Plotke.

She found Nate sitting in the waiting room and greeted him with a kiss. He seemed more nervous than she did. Though she felt some anxiety, she was more excited about actually having a sex life again. She tried to abstain from masturbating but merely managed to cut it down. Now she only played with herself before bed and when she woke in the morning. She was amazed at how much more time she had every day. She did note her previous habits on the questionnaire they both had to fill out. This one was much more personal than Blanchard's had been. She did answer every question honestly and hoped Nate did the same.

Cynthia had been worried that the therapist might be an older person like her grandmother which would make it difficult to open up. She was relieved when Glenda turned out to be only a little older than herself. The therapist had an easy manner about her and she was immediately comfortable, she hoped Nate was too and wouldn't have a problem working with a woman. Glenda explained the ground rules for the session, everything would be on the table and there could be no secrets. Each of them would have to accept what was said and be willing to respect the other person's feelings.

"I've spoken to Dave Blanchard ," Glenda said. "He indicated there may be some communication issues but that's not at all unusual. I understand what happened between you and I believe that what you had before can not only be brought back, it can be even better."

Nate and Cynthia smiled at each other and squeezed hands. Glenda went over some of the facts to confirm them and asked questions to fill in the blanks. She jotted a few notes and looked up at them.

"Cynthia, I am concerned about your masturbation habits. You seem to be using self-gratification as a substitute for intimacy."

"I've cut way down." She turned to Nate, "I was doing it a lot."

"Like every day?"

"More like six, seven times a day."

"What? I had no idea."

"Let's move on from that," Glenda said.

"Nate, let's start with you. Tell me about you first memorable sexual encounter with your wife."

"Well, we dated for a while but she wouldn't let me do much. I felt like a teenager again. She eventually let me touch her and took care of me a couple of times. Then on New Year's Eve she performed oral sex on me and we had intercourse later that night."

Glenda put down her pen and held her hand up to stop him. Cynthia looked from her to Nate and back to Glenda again and she saw a wry smile on the therapist's face.

"Nate," Glenda said, "I've heard it all, seen it all and probably done it all. There's no need to sugarcoat it. Allow me to translate: Cynthia jerked you off a couple of times, gave you a blowjob on New Year's and then you fucked her brains out. Is that about it?"

Cynthia laughed as Nate turned beet red. Glenda Plotke is her kind of woman.

"From now on," Glenda said, "if she sucked you dick say so, if you ate her pussy say it, if you fucked her up the ass own that motherfucker. Got it?"

"Yes ma'am."

"Good, now let's try again."

"Okay," Nate said. "She let me play with her tits and gave me a couple of hand jobs but it really began for us when she sucked my cock on New Year's Eve with all her friends listening in. How's that?"

"Good. Her friends were listening in?"

"Yup"

Cynthia listened as Nate explained what happened. It made her sound incredibly brazen but she really hadn't orchestrated it. She told Kelly what she was planning to do but, Kelly being Kelly and quite inebriated, told everyone and staged the kitchen scene.

"Cynthia," Glenda said, "was that your first memorable recollection?"

"No, it was before that. I really liked Nate and was afraid of repeating past mistakes. I thought if I gave in right away he would lose interest like other guys had. It drove me crazy because I wanted to fuck him the day I met him."

Cynthia looked over at Nate. He was beaming at her. She'd never told him that before and wondered why.

She continued. "We were kissing and he slipped his hand up my shirt. I intended to stop him but couldn't, I didn't let him go any further than that though. One day we were at the park – the one with the lake – it was warm for December and we made out for a while on a picnic bench. He played with my tits and I knew he wanted to fuck, and so did I. But I'd already decided I was going to wait until New Year's."

Nate was looking at her like he had no idea. Cynthia realized why he didn't, once again, she never told him.

"I made him stop, he must of thought I was such a prude. We got up and started to walk and I saw the outline of his cock on his jeans and my pussy got so wet. We walked to the lake, the whole time I kept glancing at his crotch. When we reached the shore – we were the only ones there – I looked again and it was still hard, I was losing my mind."

"You're doing good, go on," Glenda prodded.

"We kissed again and as we did I lowered his zipper and undid the button. I still remember the look on his face. I pulled his pants down just enough to get his cock out. It was the most beautiful thing I had ever seen. It was huge! It was so hard and throbbing, I remember how it felt in my hand. I told him to look at the water while I stroked him. I wanted to put it in my mouth but I was saving *that* for the big day. When he came

117

it shot so far and there was so much of it. I wanted to swallow every drop but I couldn't. I did manage to get a little on my fingers and when he wasn't looking I licked it off. It was delicious."

Cynthia watched Glenda scribbling furiously and wondered if she was writing a book. Nate just looked at her in amazement.

"You did that again?" Glenda asked.

"Oh God, I was so horny. I was ready to scrap the New Year's plans but thanks to Nate I didn't have to."

"Huh?" Nate said.

"Don't you remember? It was in the car, we were going to a party. We were kissing, he was feeling my boobs, so I took it out. I stroked that beautiful thing and was just about to put it in my mouth when he started to cum. This was one time I was happy when he came too soon."

Nate shook his head. "I had no idea. I thought you were just jerking me off to keep me happy."

Glenda put her pen down and looked at her watch. She indicated that their time was just about up and scheduled another appointment for the following week.

"I understand you're have a date tonight, that's good. I'm going to work out a game plan for the two of you. In the meantime, no sex. You can kiss and fondle but no touching below the waist. Nate, jerk off if you have to and Cynthia...well I don't need to tell you."

They walked to their cars with spring in their step. They reached her car and kissed. Nate felt her boob through her shirt.

"Easy cowboy...you haven't even bought me dinner yet."

"How about I move back in?"

Cynthia smiled slyly. "No way, I won't live with a guy I'm not fucking."

# Chapter Twenty-One

Nate was much more relaxed going into this session with Glenda Plotke. The first time he had no idea what to expect and he was a bit tentative when talking to her as if he was afraid to offend her. Not any more, not after she set him straight. He couldn't wait to get on to the next step and was anxious to see what sort of game plan the therapist had in mind. Cynthia, sitting next to him, certainly must have felt the same.

Their date the week before was fantastic. They had a nice dinner and just talked, really talked. They both realized that was something they hadn't done in a very long time. One thing they both agreed on was that they would abstain from alcohol during these dates to avoid losing control. They readily admitted that they needed to fuck but they followed Glenda's instructions to the letter. They made out a little, in the car like they used to, but that was it. Nate didn't even try to cop a feel.

They were ushered into Glenda's office right at the appointed time. They each gave their version of the prior week's events. They were asked about their masturbation since the last session a week prior. Cynthia said she played with herself a total of twelve times, far less than normal. Nate felt like a slacker because he had only jerked off four times. Glenda didn't seem at all surprised by either answer and suspected that she was rarely caught off guard.

"I see you two had a good week," Glenda said. "I assume you feel you're ready for the next step?"

Nate looked at Cynthia then they both looked toward the therapist and nodded. Nate noticed Cynthia leaning forward in the chair so he mirrored her action as he waited to hear what was next.

"Cynthia, I see your masturbation has subsided a bit and is no longer off the charts. However, I still think this next assignment may be tough for you. Nate, you should have no problem."

"What do we need to do?" Nate asked.

Glenda looked directly at Cynthia. "First it's what not to do. You are not to masturbate for forty-eight hours."

Nate heard an audible gasp from his wife. He still couldn't wrap his head around how frequently she played with herself. He remembered doing it a lot when he was a teenager but even then twice in the same day was rare.

"Next," Glenda continued. "Each of you will masturbate in front of the other. The one masturbating is to be completely naked, the one watching fully clothed. The idea is to pay attention to how your partner pleasures themselves. You are not to talk or interact in any way, just masturbate the same way you would if you were alone. There should also be a minimum of a sixty minute break in between. I suggest a shower or a walk, any way to break it up rather than simply going after each other. Any question about that?"

"Just one," Cynthia said. "Do we have to wait another week to find out what's next?"

Glenda smiled. "No. I have a plan for you to follow. After our one-on-one sessions I realize that both of you have issues communicating so I tried to make it easy for you."

Glenda passed two sealed envelopes to each of them. Nate's were marked "Date 2" and "Date 4." He assumed Cynthia had one and three. He felt a jolt of excitement as he wondered what was in the envelopes.

"As you may have guessed," Glenda said, "you are not to open the envelopes. Continue with your twice a week dates. Prior to dinner or whatever you plan to do you open the appropriate envelope. Don't tell your partner what it says, just follow the instructions. Please understand, you are not to go beyond the written instructions."

"Then what?" Nate asked.

"You come back in two weeks. At that time, assuming you followed the instructions properly, you'll get your next assignment. Trust me, you'll really like that one."

Two nights later they had takeout at the house. It was the first time Nate had been back home other than to pick up his mail. Cynthia seemed a bit antsy and Nate assumed it was because she had gone more than two days without an orgasm. He was looking forward to this. Though his wife touched herself at times when they had sex, he had never really watched her masturbate. He didn't think she had seen him either. He would stroke himself to get hard and once in a while finish himself off by hand, but he couldn't recall jerking off from start to finish in front of her.

They were done with dinner. He put the cartons with the unfinished portions in the refrigerator while she loaded the dishwasher. They had the living room set up so that the one performing could sit in the recliner while the observer sat on the sofa. They decided that she would go first so she left the room to get ready. She returned about five minutes later carrying a vibrator and wearing a robe. He sat down and waited while she walked to the chair and paused.

"You ready?" he asked.

"Yeah, but I feel a little nervous."

"Don't be, just enjoy yourself."

Cynthia looked at him and let the robe fall to the floor. Nate hadn't seen her naked since before he went on his trip. She was beautiful. Her boobs looked huge and looked so sexy, her nipples erect. She sat in the chair and spread her legs slightly. He noticed she had trimmed for the occasion. Not one of her dark pubes was out of place and he felt himself get hard as she slowly ran her fingers through them. He was going to enjoy this, he just hoped he didn't cum in his pants while he watched.

# Chapter Twenty-Two

Cynthia was feeling a little self-conscious. She knew that masturbating in front of Nate was a way of symbolically stating that there were no secrets between them. She understood that, but this was an activity that she considered her private and very personal domain. It was the one thing that was hers and hers alone. Still she understood perfectly why the therapist wanted them to do it and she intended to do it right and perform as if Nate was not watching. She just hoped she could actually do it.

She last masturbated when she returned from, Glenda's office two days ago. She had a few close calls since then. Cynthia's fingers moved toward her clit out of reflex when she went to bed and again when she woke up. As difficult as it was, she abstained for almost fifty hours to this point. Taking a deep breath, she put her vibrator down on the table next to the recliner and let her robe fall to the floor. She heard a sharp intake of air from Nate and was pleased that she turned him on. Trying to guess the contents of Glenda's note for date number one was the thing that was turning her on. *What could it be?*

Glenda met with each of them privately the day before their last joint session. The therapist wanted to see them alone to probe the details of what had happened and to try to get a handle on who they were as people without being worried about what they may say with their spouse present. Cynthia went into great detail about her tryst with Zach and the events that led up to it. Through a series of questions and the answers to the questionnaire Glenda sought to determine why Cynthia could be a take-charge type of person like she was on New Year's some of the time and yet be very passive at others. Glenda's theory was that Cynthia really was somewhat dominant but had been conditioned to believe that women shouldn't be like that. Glenda's goal was to get Cynthia to allow her natural dominance to assert itself.

Cynthia settled into the recliner and parted her legs so that Nate would have a good view, then she closed her eyes and tried to forget he was there. She slowly ran her fingers through the pubes she had trimmed that very morning. She lightly tugged at the hair before the fingers moved to spread her labia. Rubbing the lips sent an electric charge through her clit. Moisture started to flow and Cynthia brought her fingers to her mouth to lick them before returning to her pussy. She fingered her pussy lips, then her clit, back to the lips then the clit, which was now very swollen. She reached for her vibrator and switched it on and started working herself. She vibrated her clit then eased it inside her vagina and moved it slowly in and out. He left hand massaged her boobs and squeezed the nipples. She had a couple of mini orgasms as she passed the vibrator over her clit. She'd been working it for at least ten minutes and could feel the big one start to build. Images flooded her brain and she imagined she could feel hands all over her body, tongues on her tits, her pussy, her anus. She remembered Zach eating her asshole and her body began to shudder.

"*Arrggghhhh!* Oh yes...yes....."

Cynthia switched off the vibrator. She allowed herself to catch her breath before she opened her eyes. Nate was staring at her wide-eyed, the bulge in his pants impossible to miss. She gave him a sheepish smile.

"Wow," he said. "That was hot. You do that to yourself like six times a day? Every day?"

"Sometimes more."

"Wow, that's like...wow. "

"You have no idea."

# Chapter Twenty-Three

After Cynthia got dressed they took a walk around the neighborhood. As per Glenda's instructions they didn't talk about the masturbation that he had just witnessed. They either talked about mundane things or just continued on silently until they returned home about forty minutes later. Nate went to the bedroom to get ready for his turn. He stripped and slipped into a robe. Remembering how neatly trimmed Cynthia's pubes had been he ran a comb through his and snipped away any unruly hairs. When a full hour had passed since his wife finished her made his way to the living room.

In his solo meeting with Glenda he recounted everything that occurred including Tamara's theory that he was really submissive. He explained how he followed Tamara's instructions without hesitation, even the ones he swore he wouldn't. Glenda also asked him to tell her about his most memorable encounters with Cynthia and pointed out to him that the ones he liked best were those where his wife had been dominant. She also pointed out that though Tamara had done a lot of things he liked, she had done them on her own terms.

"There was one thing I didn't like," Nate said.

"What was that?"

He hesitated briefly. "She pissed in my face."

"But you let her, didn't you?"

"No, I didn't."

Nate explained how Tamara had pinned him down before dousing him with the golden shower.

"Are you sure you didn't like it?"

"Of course I didn't."

"Close your eyes for a minute," Glenda said. "Now think back to that moment. Sure, there was a bit of shock because you didn't expect it. Try to recall how it felt...really think. When she let you up, what was your strongest emotion? *Were* you angry?"

Nate recalled the stream hitting his face, the warmth, the saltiness. Trying not to swallow. The taste as he licked her pussy clean.

Glenda looked into his eyes. "Be honest now, what one word would you use to describe how you felt at that moment?"

"Humiliated."

Nate's mind returned to his performance. He reached the living room and Cynthia was waiting on the sofa. She'd kicked off her shoes and her legs were curled under her, her hands hugging her knees. She had the look of a kid on Christmas morning and he was her present. There was no way he could put on the kind of show she did and he hoped she wouldn't be disappointed. He reached the chair, took off his robe and tossed it aside. He didn't even attempt the seductiveness of letting it fall to the floor the way she had. He settled back in the chair, adjusted his testicles and stretched his penis which was just starting to react. He played with his balls and lightly touched his cock until he was about halfway erect. He ran his finger in a circular motion around the head. His eyes were closed the entire time.

His fingers encircled the shaft at the base and he tugged very gently. This wasn't a maintenance jerk and he wanted to last a long time. He sped up as he became fully hard but still wasn't touching the most sensitive part. He threw one leg over the arm of the chair and got into a steady rhythm as moved up to the more sensitive area of the shaft. When he was close to ejaculating he stopped. His cock was throbbing and a little semen appeared on the tip. When it was safe to do so he resumed and stroked again until he reached the edge once more. He repeated this two more times but on the second he realized he had reached the point of no return. He tightened his grip and quickened his pace as he felt his balls tightening. His cock started to pulsate and a split second later a large stream of semen shot almost a foot into the air.

"*Urrgghhh!*"

Nate kept stroking but loosened his grip and slowed the intensity until the last bit of semen came out. His ejaculate had reached as far as his chest and covered his stomach. He gulped for air until caught his breath, then used a washcloth to clean himself up. He looked at Cynthia – she was beaming.

"Wow," she said. "That was *sooo* hot, I'm soaked. Next time you're going to jerk off let me know so I can watch. Wow!"

The following night they were on their date. This time it was hamburgers at a pub with a strict two beer limit. Cynthia was more animated than usual, obviously excited by the content of her envelope which she stubbornly refused to reveal. They discussed how hot it had been to watch each other masturbate and said it was something they should do once in a while. Nate also brought up the subject of his homecoming and Cynthia agreed it was almost time, but not quite yet. She felt like they were dating and getting to know each other all over again. She did promise it would be soon.

Dinner was finished and they went to the car. He led her to the passenger door and kissed her as he opened it for her. She got in and he went around on entered the driver side. He went to start the car but she grabbed his shirt collar and pulled him to her. Their lips met and Nate felt her tongue as it probed his. Her hand went to his crotch and easily found his erection. Without breaking their kiss her fingers located and lowered his zipper and skillfully unbuttoned his pants. She tugged them open and slipped her hand inside his briefs.

"Take them down," she said.

They were directly under a street lamp and he was fully illuminated.

"Someone might see."

"Lucky them. Now take them down."

He lowered them to mid thigh so his cock was exposed but he could still pull them up quickly if they were interrupted.

"All the way."

"But..."

"Just do it."

He pushed them down to his ankles and sat back in the seat. She twisted sideways and he hoped she was going to blow him. Her posture told him that wasn't the case. She reached across the sit and reached the "recline" lever and eased him back to about a forty-five degree angle. Her hand circled his cock and he thought he was going to explode, she hadn't touched him in weeks.

"Now look straight ahead or shut your eyes if you want. Concentrate on how it feels and nothing else. Got it?"

"Yes ma'am."

He closed his eyes as her hand went to work.

# Chapter Twenty-Four

Cynthia was just as excited as the first time she'd ever touched Nate's manhood. She felt its firmness, as if for the first time, as she encircled its girth. Warmth resonated through her fingers which each throb as she slid her hand up and down the silky-smooth length. Nate sighed with pleasure as she applied more pressure and the skin moved up and down with her hand. She paused frequently so he wouldn't cum too quickly, each time she did she loosened her grip and marveled at the beauty of his penis. She loved the head and the softness of the skin on the top half of the shaft and the way the top looked different from the lower part. She still considered it the nicest cock she had ever seen.

Glenda's note had begged to be opened but Cynthia resisted the temptation and didn't unseal it until the proper time. She understood the therapist's intent and would follow the directions, it was really so simple:

End of date instructions:
In a semi-public place you are to perform a hand job
Try to recapture the spirit of that first time
Assert yourself as we discussed
There is to be no sexual contact beyond this


She watched her fingers as they glided across his cock. Nate started to squirm and breathe heavily. She tightened her grip and cupped his balls while squeezing. She felt them go tight against his body and she had to fight the urge to take him in her mouth. He grunted as he arched his back and a stream of semen shot out of him. She gradually slowed her strokes as the last of his ejaculate oozed out and down across her fingers. Using a tissue she had handy she wiped away the sticky goo, when she was sure he wasn't looking she licked a wad of it off her fingers and savored the taste. She wondered why she'd developed the habit of spitting it out when she sucked him off and vowed that from now on she wouldn't waste a drop of that precious fluid.

Nate gathered himself and pulled his pants up. He leaned over to kiss her and tried to squeeze her breasts but pushed him away.

"That was awesome." Nate reached for her boobs again. "You don't know how much I want you."

She pushed his hand away. "Forget it buddy, it ain't happening until we're told it's okay."

"I don't know how much longer I can take this."

"Deal with it. Now take me home so I can play with myself."

After Nate dropped her off Cynthia poured herself a glass of wine. She'd had two with dinner but was so worked up that she needed another in order to relax. When the glass was finished she changed into her nightshirt and went to bed. She opened her nightstand and selected her favorite vibrator – the one that was about the same size as Nate – and buzzed herself to sleep.

For the next two days she tried to imagine what Nate's instructions might be. Would Glenda have him recreate one of their early encounters, or would it be something different. The first two times she gave him hand jobs and the third was when she sucked him off in the pantry. After the blowjob they went to his place and fucked like crazy but she was sure Glenda wouldn't have them at that point so quickly. They did, after all, have envelopes for the next two dates as well. She did realize one thing, she was the aggressive one early on in their relationship. Cynthia was walking through the house when she stopped in her tracks – she always *had* been the assertive one. That trait disappeared after the miscarriage and Nate didn't know how to deal with it. What he called "giving her space" was really a way of saying he was waiting for her to take charge again. *My God, it really is all my fault.*

Cynthia was feeling a little down as she walked around in her robe getting ready for their date that night. Since they started on Glenda's program she'd been so excited and optimistic but her epiphany totally changed her mood. She even considered the idea of calling Nate and cancelling and waiting until she was in a better frame of mind. She decided to put her feet up for a few minutes in the hope that her mood might change. She closed her eyes and tried to relax. Within minutes she was opening her robe and fingering herself. As became very wet and started to tingle a little she abruptly stopped and jumped up. She moved across the room and stood in front of the mirror staring at her reflection.

*You fucked this up – you fix it. Stop playing with your goddamn pussy all the time and fix your fucking relationship. That amazing man loves you – so fucking let him you stupid cunt!*

She closed her eyes and took several deep breaths. When she opened them again she looked at her face and forced a smile. The strained facial muscles relaxed as the grin became a wicked one – *what's in that envelope?*

They were at a nice Italian restaurant they both loved but hadn't been to in quite a while. She felt a lot better and was glad she hadn't cancelled. Nate was being very attentive but he also seemed very nervous, she assumed it had to do with the contents of his envelope.

"Can't you at least give me a hint?" she asked.

"You didn't."

"I know but...well, you seem so nervous."

"I...I am a little, weren't you?"

"Maybe a little." She sipped her wine. "Can't you tell me anything?"

"Well..."

"C'mon, tell me!"

"Just this, we'll be going back to my room."

Now Cynthia was really curious. "Your room?"

"Unfortunately, we won't be fucking."

"Damn!"

They shared a piece of cheesecake for desert and lingered over cappuccino. Conversation was easy and they really enjoyed themselves. The check arrived and Nate paid it. As they walked to his car she sensed the return of his nervousness but didn't comment. They drove in silence to the extended stay hotel he called home, prior to this she had never been there. Cynthia realized she had no idea how he'd been living and felt a twinge of guilt since they'd both strayed yet he was the one suffering by living in this place for almost a month. They walked in through the lobby and to his room. She thought it was cute. It had a kitchenette, living area and a separate bedroom. She was surprised to see what occupied the area in front of the television – a massage table.

Nate handed her a robe. "Go take a quick shower and come back wearing only this."

She took the robe. "That's a sneaky way to get a girl to take her clothes off."

Cynthia stripped and jumped in the shower. She was surprised, and happy, to see her favorite body wash waiting for her. As she lathered herself she made sure her pussy was clean since she assumed he was going to play with it or, hopefully, eat it. She hadn't had a massage in ages and intended to enjoy it even though Nate wasn't a pro. She dried herself off, slipped on the robe and returned to the other room where her husband was waiting for her.

Nate patted the table. "Hop on."

Facing away from him, she slipped off the robe and lay face down on the table with her arms outstretched. The table had a cutout for her face so she didn't have to twist her neck in an uncomfortable position. When she was settled Nate covered her ass with a towel.

Cynthia laughed. "What's with the towel? You've seen my ass before."

"I need to be able to concentrate."

"Concentrate?"

"Yeah, I read a book on how to do this. I hope I do okay."

He started slowly kneading her shoulders and then her neck. He worked his fingers through her scalp and moved down to her arms. He took his time and was taking this very seriously.  Cynthia was really getting into it thoroughly enjoying his efforts. He bypassed the towel, and her ass, and went to her feet. He worked one then the other before moving up to her calves. When he reached her thighs she felt her pussy moisten and realized she was extremely horny. *This better include a happy ending!*

His hands moved up and down her hamstrings and she thought he actually knows what he's doing. He moved his fingers up the inside of her thighs and she shivered as they came close to her pussy. Unfortunately they never touched. His hands moved back to her thighs and then slipped under the towel. She reached her hand back, grabbed the cloth and tossed it aside. He worked her buttocks for what she thought was a very long time. The he started to kiss her cheeks, right one, left and right again. Up and down he kissed, mixing in a few licks with the tongue.

"*Oh yes!*"

# Chapter Twenty-Five

Nate made every effort to do his very best. Never before had he done more than a perfunctory back rub. When instructed to perform a massage he decided to locate a book suitable for an amateur that would enable him, at the very least, to give one that didn't totally suck. He even looked into renting a massage table and asked the concierge at his hotel where he might find one. To his surprise and delight he was told that the hotel had one on site and, with the help of a generous tip, he could borrow it for a few hours. It was rolled into his room and he set it up in the center of the living area after moving the coffee table out of the way.

The book used pictures to demonstrate various techniques and he spent a good deal of time studying the pages. Most of it seemed fairly straightforward and though he wasn't really able to practice, he at least had a sense of a sequence to follow instead of trying to wing it. It was the latter part of Glenda's instructions – where he was at this point – that was a bit troubling. The book made no real mention of it and it was not something he'd ever done, or even had an inkling to try. He hoped he could do it satisfactorily and not be grossed out. The instructions were explicit and there was no room for misinterpretation.

End of date instructions:

In a private location perform a back massage

There is to be no touching of breasts, or vagina

or any contact at all with the pubic triangle

The massage is to be one hour in length with

30 minutes devoted to the worship of her posterior

This is to include a *minimum* of 20 minutes spent

licking her anus

The last line is what troubled him. Never had he licked Cynthia's, or anyone else's, asshole. He was afraid he wouldn't be able to do it and wasn't sure she would even like it. He had determined to give it his best and began the way the book suggested. He even placed a towel over her ass, though she thought it was funny it did help him focus on giving a good massage.

He massaged her neck, her shoulders, her scalp. He worked her back, then her feet and moved up her legs. As his fingers kneaded the muscles of her thighs she parted her legs a little more and he caught a glimpse of her pussy and was instantly erect. He slipped his hands under the towel and caressed her buttocks. Though totally without droop, her ass was very soft and he loved the feel of it. Cynthia's hand reached back, grabbed the towel and tossed it aside, he was about to remove it anyway. He spent a couple of minutes on her cheeks as she cooed softly. He gently spread them apart and looked at the puckered pink spot that was her anus. Rather than dive right in he kissed her butt cheeks, alternating between right and left. As he stole a glance at the bedside clock, he buried his face between them and his tongue touched her hole.

Cynthia inhaled sharply. "*Oh yes!*"

Encouraged by his wife's reaction he continued to lick. His concerns about the taste quickly dissipated as he realized that it wasn't bad at all. He tried to do it like licking a pussy, moving his tongue all around. Cynthia was squirming a bit as he tongued her and arched her ass back into him several times. Emboldened by this, he forced his tongue in and out her anus which caused her to squirm even more. Her bucking turned into a shudder.

"*Arrrgggghh!*"

He kept licking as her orgasm subsided and he realized that she had reached her hand down to finger herself as he ate her ass. The instructions clearly stated that he couldn't touch her clit but it didn't say she couldn't – not that he could have stopped her. Looking at the clock he saw he had gone five minutes past his allotted time so he slowed his pace and stopped after about another minute. When she realized he was done she sat up and dangled her legs over the side of the table. He was so turned on by looking at her and what he had done to her, but he wasn't going to attempt anything further.

Cynthia licked her lips. "That...that was so unbelievably hot. I never knew I would enjoy that so much."

"I'll have to add that to my repertoire."

"I'll say, that was so awesome."

After dropping Cynthia at the house, Nate went back to his hotel. Before returning the massage table he decided to use it for one more activity. He stripped down, jumped on and stroked himself. He lay there recalling what he had just done and decided that eating ass wasn't bad after all, he actually enjoyed it or, more to the point, she loved how much she enjoyed it. He masturbated long and slow and didn't ejaculate for almost twenty minutes. When he was done he folded the table and moved it to the hallway and called the front desk to have them take it away. He wondered where he could buy one for the house.

Their next date was coming up but Nate was getting impatient. He was tired of living out of a suitcase and wanted to go home. He was sure Cynthia was ready for him to come back as well. He liked the way Glenda's game plan was progressing for them but wondered if they could accelerate it a little. There was no question that they were getting back together, so why should they wait? By the same token he realized that this phase would be over within a week anyway. He would ride this out but if the next step didn't include moving back he would certainly protest. In the meantime he was anxious to find out what was next.

Cynthia decided on pizza and a movie. It was her envelope so she got to choose when, what and where their date would be. As usual she wouldn't discuss what she had planned. The movie she selected turned out to be a drama, not the "chick flick" he'd feared. Before the film they went to their favorite pizza place and split a medium pie with half pepperoni and half spinach. He refused to consider mushrooms for fear that they would migrate onto his side of the pizza. When she jokingly suggested anchovies he said if she went that way the reconciliation was off. They had a great time at dinner and held hands throughout the movie. When the picture was over she led him out of the theater still holding his hand.

They reached the hallway and Nate started to turn left to exit the multiplex but Cynthia turned the opposite way and pulled him along. They walked against the flow of people leaving the building and he assumed she was heading for the ladies room. Instead she kept walking down the hallway toward the emergency exit but stopped short of the door. Cynthia looked back over her shoulder and down the hallway before pulling him into an empty theater. The door shut behind them enveloping them in darkness. She walked carefully down the aisle past several rows of seats, the turned and leaned against the wall while pulling him to her. Nate felt her warm breath as she brought her lips to his. They kissed passionately for several minutes though Nate kept listening for the opening of the door. Cynthia finally broke free and took his hand again. He felt the seatbacks as she led him to the middle of a row.

"Sit down."

Nate did as she said and settled into the seat, it was the oversize reclining variety the newer cinemas have now. Cynthia dropped to her knees and started unfastening his belt, undoing his button and lowering his zipper. She tugged at his pants as he protested but he lifted his ass off the seat so she could get them down. When they were around his ankles she took his very erect cock into her hand and lowered her head toward it.

"Someone might walk in," he said.

"So let them."

"They'll see us."

"Good for them, I just hope they don't think I'm sucking them off too."

# Chapter Twenty-Six

Cynthia's eyes were adjusting to the dark. There was just enough light filtering and there was a small sliver of emergency lighting as well. The outline of Nate's cock was clearly visible as she held it and massaged his testicles. He moaned very softly as she took him into her mouth as she savored the moment. She forgot how much she loved doing this. She'd been giving him a very poor facsimile of a blow job for almost two years now. There hadn't been any thought to making him feel good, just getting him off as quickly as possible so he'd leave her alone for another week. In reality she was just jerking him off with her mouth.

His movements told her he was close to ejaculating so she eased off and let him get back under control. When she was sure the pause had been long enough she resumed licking the head of his cock. She wanted to build this one up so it would be huge. Cynthia hoped she implemented the last part of her instructions properly and that Nate liked it. She was so excited when she read them that she had the instant urge – which she resisted – to masturbate. She just wanted to be sure her timing was right:

End of date instructions:

Again in a semi-public, but safe, setting

Perform oral sex that mirrors that first New Year's

As he nears ejaculation you are to finger his anus

Just prior to orgasm you are to finger fuck him until ejaculation is complete


Her concern was timing, she feared using her finger too late or too soon. She took him into her mouth again and slowly worked him back to the point of orgasm. While sucking on him she discretely wet her own finger and approached his anus. She looked at him and even in the dark she could see his eyes were closed. He started moaning a little louder and she knew he had totally forgotten where he was. It was time. As she picked up the pace of her sucking her finger touched his hole lightly. When he squirmed a little she added pressure. She tasted a little bit of cum and knew he was right there. Her finger pushed in to the first digit and he moaned again. Nate started pushing against her finger and she inserted all the way and began finger fucking him just as he let out a groan and a blast of hot semen shot against the back of her throat. His cock was erupting and his ejaculate seemed like it wouldn't stop. She almost gagged and was about to pull away when he was finally empty. Her mouth came off and she stroked him very lightly by hand teasing out the last few drops which she greedily licked away.

She rested her head on his thigh. "Seems like I'm not the only one who likes their ass played with."

"Certainly seems that way."

Nate stood up and Cynthia helped him fasten his pants. She took his hand led him up the inclined aisle toward the door. They had just about reached it when it opened and an usher with a flashlight  stood their looking at them.

He held the door for them. "You shouldn't be in here."

"It's okay, we're leaving now. I was just giving my husband a blowjob."

Back home that night Cynthia kept replaying the scene in her mind, she had such a blast. The risk of being caught heightened everything for her. She'd forgotten how often she did things like that in public places and marveled at how Glenda's instructions helped her get back in touch with that part of her. Nate was always a little uncomfortable with it and that too was a big part of the turn-on for her. He was shocked when she made that comment to the usher. It had been a great night, she was so glad she hadn't cancelled.

Two days later she was getting ready for the last date Glenda had prescribed and wondered what Nate's instructions were. Hers had simply been recreating what she'd done before but his weren't. Nothing obvious came to mind so she tried not to think about it and just let the evening happen. The date itself was dinner and drinks at a pub, after that she had no idea. He picked her up right on time and went to eat. Cynthia saw that Nate was very relaxed this time so it must be something he's comfortable with. She certainly understood the angst he felt the last time but he'd come through with flying colors and she expected no less this time.

They finished their meal and were having the last of their drinks when she made the effort to at least get a hint of what was going to happen.

Cynthia reached across the table for his hand. "I assume you're not going to tell me."

"Of course not, you know the drill."

"Can you tell me where?"

"You'll find out soon enough," he said. "But if you must know you're going to my room again."

"Oooh, another massage."

"Sorry, I gave the table back."

"Maybe we're..."

"We won't be fucking either."

"Damn!"

Cynthia scanned Nate's room as they entered looking for any telltale signs but nothing was out of the ordinary. He grabbed a couple of cold beers out of the fridge and handed her one. She actually felt nervous, which she thought was absurd. Nate went into the bathroom while she waited on the sofa but he returned a minute or two later looking exactly the same. He did, however, go over to the bed and strip off the bed spread and toss the decorative pillows aside. She looked up at him and waited for instructions.

He grabbed her hand and pulled her up off the couch. He led her to the bed and sat her down as he sat beside her. She kicked off her shoes as he kissed her and started to unfasten the buttons of her blouse. Cynthia felt her nipples get hard as she helped him slip it off. The back of his fingers ran across the fabric of her bra and across her nipples causing her to shiver. He pushed her back on the bed and unfastened her jeans. She arched her back lifting her ass off the bed allowing him to slip he pants off. Now wearing only her bra and panties she scooted up to the pillows and lay back, her mind racing in anticipation.

"I thought we weren't going to fuck," she said.

"We're not and, alas, I will not be naked."

"But I will? Doesn't seem fair."

"Indeed it doesn't."

Cynthia's eyes followed him as he opened the drawer on the dresser and took something out. He went to the closet and returned with a plastic bag but she couldn't tell what it might contain. Her horniness turned into curiosity as she tried to decipher what he was doing. He handed her the object he took from the draw, she looked at it a moment before realizing what it was.

"A blindfold?"

He shook his head. "Just put it on."

She slipped it over her head taking care not to get her hair bunched up in the band. She leaned back on the bed and heard him doing something in the corner. He came back to the bed and slipped something over her right wrist, then the left. He did the same to each ankle. He had her lean forward so he could unfasten her bra, he removed it as she dropped back on the bed, her boobs slid toward her side. He took one wrist and pulled it to the side, she heard a click and realized she was fastened to something.

"You're tying me up?"

"Just following orders."

Her arms were securely fastened but not uncomfortably so. He pulled at her panties, tugging them down. She lifted her ass off the bed so he could slip them off. Next he secured her ankles and she was totally helpless as she waited for his next move. She felt him get off the bed and heard him moving to the door. There was a click and what light she could see under the blindfold disappeared. A few seconds later he returned to the bed and sat beside her. She felt his jeans against her thigh and saw that he wasn't kidding about staying dressed.

Cynthia felt Nate stretch out next to her. One hand cupped her head as he began to nibble on her neck. She heard a gasp and realized it was coming from her. He kissed her skin as he made his way down to her chest. His left hand caressed one breast while he started kissing the other and sucking the very erect nipple.

Cynthia squirmed. "Oh God, yes!"

He switched boobs for a short time then started moving south. Her thighs quivered as he kissed around the outside of her pubic hair. She anticipated his tongue on her pussy but he moved right past and started kissing her thighs and slowly working down to her ankles and feet. One by one he sucked her toes – he had never done that before. She willed him higher as he began working his way back up. She felt the juices running down her legs and thought she might cum without even being touched. The blindfold caused her to focus solely on the feeling since she couldn't see what was happening. He almost reached her pussy when she started thrusting it in the direction of his face. She bit her lip as his tongue reached her labia and licked them apart. She squealed when her reached her clit.

"*Ahhh...yessss!*"

# Chapter Twenty-Seven

Nate was ecstatic. Cynthia's reaction was exactly what he expected but he was still pleased when it actually happened. She had two big orgasms, an untold number of smaller ones and another that was absolutely off the charts. She was moaning, gasping, crying out, thrashing about and constantly straining against the restraints. He had been anxious when he opened the envelope but extremely relieved when he saw what it said:

End of date instructions:

This is to be performed in a private place

You are to blindfold and restrain your wife

She is to be fully nude while you remain clothed

Perform cunnilingus for a minimum of one hour

There is to be no vaginal penetration with

anything other than your tongue

He was thirty minutes past the minimum and had no desire to stop when he glanced at the clock for the first time. Cynthia certainly made no effort to stop him. He did pause now and then to allow he to catch her breath but that was it. The only uncertainty was whether he was allowed to touch more than her pussy. The instructions didn't forbid it so he assumed it was okay. He just wanted to devour every inch of her and that's what he had done.

Nate almost came in his pants more than once, that was something he hadn't done since he was a hormonal train wreck of a teenager. He took his time exploring her neck, breasts, thighs, and pussy as if for the first time. Sucking her toes was a new wrinkle that just occurred but the way she reacted assured that it certainly wouldn't be the last time he did that. She finally seemed totally spent as he approached the two hour mark so he stopped. He unfastened the restraints and removed the blindfold. She sat up and grabbed the beer, which had to be warm by this point, and took several big gulps.

She ran her fingers through her hair. "That was....that....that was so fucking awesome."

"Trust me, the pleasure was all mine."

Her hand reached out and touched his still erect cock through his pants. He almost came on the spot. She shifted her position and reached for his belt with both hands. He pushed her away.

"I want to suck your cock."

"No, we're not supposed to go that far."

"Damn it Nate, I don't care."

"Cynthia, we..."

"Drop your goddamn pants and give me your fucking cock – *now damn it*!"

Nate let go of her hand and let her open his pants. He kneeled on the bed as her fingers fumbled with the zipper and tugged his jeans to mid-thigh exposing his huge hard-on. Her right hand circled the base as she swiftly lowered her mouth on to him. He exploded instantly. She sucked until he stopped ejaculating. Nate was catching his breath as she opened her mouth and showed him her cum-covered tongue, then she swallowed and opened her mouth again to reveal his load was gone.

She smiled at him. "I won't tell if you don't."

"Deal"

Nate watched her as she went to the bathroom to clean herself up. He'd been ready to explode from the moment she took her clothes off. He probably hadn't cum that fast, less than fifteen seconds, since he was a teenager with a bad case of premature ejaculation. Cynthia didn't seem to mind one bit. She came back into the room, still naked, and grabbed a couple of beers out of the fridge and sat on the sofa. He sat in the chair across from her as they drank their brews. He was admiring her body and couldn't wait until they were sleeping in the same bed again.

Cynthia spread her legs a little and held the beer bottle against her pussy. "I need to cool this thing off. You were incredible."

"Glad to be of service."

"Nate, I'm tired of this. I want you to come back home."

"We see Glenda tomorrow. We've completed her program, this phase anyway. Hopefully that's the next step."

"If it isn't I want you to come back anyway."

# Chapter Twenty-Eight

Cynthia and Nate sat in adjacent chairs across from Glenda Plotke. They held hands across the small gap between the seats and smiled at each other as they waited for Glenda to finish a telephone call. After scribbling a few notes on a pad the therapist hung up the phone and looked at them.

"By the expressions on your faces I gather things went well."

They both nodded. Cynthia was anxious to hear Glenda say they could resume living together, though she planned on doing that either way. She also wanted to know the next step and recalled Glenda's assurance that they would like it. After the four dates she had no doubt about that. The therapist reviewed something in their file for a moment before closing it and setting it back down on her desk.

"As I'm sure you surmised," Glenda said, "each of the instructions had a purpose. I would like to hear your thoughts on what it was. Let's start with date one – Cynthia?"

Cynthia cleared her throat. "You wanted me to see Nate like I did that first time, to remember how much I loved his cock."

"And?"

"I'm not sure."

"Well," Glenda said. "You took the initiative, the more aggressive role. You did it on your terms that first time while Nate was subservient. I wanted you to feel that way again. How about you Nate, what did you learn from that?"

"I realized that she wasn't doing it for me, but for her. I never understood how much she enjoyed it that first time."

"That's a start," Glenda said. "What about the second set of instructions, Nate?"

"I was worried about that," Nate said. "I wasn't sure I could do it, eat her anus, but after the start it was okay and when I saw how much she enjoyed it I got into it."

"But why did I have you do it?"

"As a way of submitting to her?"

"Good. Cynthia?"

"My God. I loved, loved, loved it! I'm not really sure why."

"Okay, perhaps because he was demonstrating his submission? Tell me about number three."

"It was a hoot!" Cynthia said. "I had such a blast doing that in public, well sort of public. It was like that first New Year's and I got such an adrenaline rush. I guess the reason was to have me take charge."

"Good. Nate?"

"I was worried about being caught but I couldn't stop her. I guess it was to show me to let her take control and just follow along."

"And what about the last time?"

"It was incredible," Nate said. "I had such a great time and I know Cynthia did too."

Cynthia interrupted him. "I cheated."

"Tell me," Glenda said.

She explained what happened after Nate ate her and also expressed her frustration and that she was losing patience. She told the therapist she wanted Nate back now. Glenda leaned back in her chair, held her hands in the steeple position, and beamed a thousand watt smile.

"Perfect!"

Cynthia looked at Nate and arched her eyebrow as if to tell him she was confused. Nate shrugged back at her and they both turned to look at Glenda.

"You guys did great and understood some of my intentions. Your extreme impatience is a sign that you're ready and hopefully you've figured out what went wrong in the first place. Here's the deal – you're both trying to be the opposite of what you really are."

"How so?" Cynthia asked.

"I've tried to explain this before. You're both trying to act the way society says you should. The man is supposed to be the alpha male and the woman his submissive mate. The two of you are totally opposite."

"And these dates were supposed to show that," Nate said.

"Precisely. Cynthia, you're happiest when you are leading the way and being daring."

"I realized that, I've always been the dominant one without really knowing it."

"Yes, and Nate you're happiest when Cynthia takes charge."

"By eating her ass?"

"Yes! That is a form of submission. You were showing her you worship her and wish to serve her, to a degree."

"But the last time I was in charge."

"Were you?"

"Wasn't I?"

"You were worshiping the queen. Tying her up allowed her to focus on the pleasure you were providing her rather than her instinctively controlling you. If she insisted that you untie her what would you have done?"

"I would have untied her."

Glenda smiled. "Of course you would have. When she broke the rules you didn't prevent her from doing so."

"She would not be stopped."

Glenda laughed. "Not by you."

Cynthia hung her head for a moment. "I...I realized something the other day."

"What was that?" Glenda asked.

"All of this was my fault."

"No it wasn't," Nate insisted.

"Yes, yes it was. I was depressed after the miscarriage, feeling sorry for myself. So I wasn't taking charge."

"That doesn't make it your fault."

"Nate, said you always tried to give me space."

"You needed it."

"That wasn't what you were doing. You were waiting for me to take the lead again because you didn't know how."

Nate looked crestfallen. "I know how..."

Cynthia covered his hand with hers. "No sweetie, you don't...and it's okay because that's not your job."

Cynthia saw that Glenda was ecstatic about her epiphany and assured her that she shouldn't blame herself, just learn from it. The therapist asked a few more questions while filling in some of the blanks for them. She told them that they now were each more aware of who they were and had a better understanding of their roles, though not completely. That would all get better with time. However, they were ready for the next, and final, step. Rather than move back in right away, Glenda suggested they go away for a couple of days. Sort of a sexual vacation. They should go to a nice hotel or resort that had a restaurant on site and provided room service. Then they should spend the entire time having sex.

Nate smiled. "A sexcation!"

"More like a fuck-cation," Cynthia retorted.

"I do have a project for you on your...er..fuck-a-thon," Glenda said. "I think you'll have a lot of fun with it."

Glenda explained what she wanted them to do and what the purpose was. She said they should consider it part of their "after-care" program. Cynthia thought it was a fantastic idea and Nate seemed to agree. They thanked Glenda and prepared to leave. As they stood up the therapist asked Nate to wait in the lobby while she spoke privately to his wife for a moment. Cynthia was curious as she sat back down. She felt the color drain from her face when Glenda explained what she wanted her to do.

"I'm not sure I could do that," Cynthia said.

"You can, I'm sure. You don't see it yet but it would be good for Nate."

"I just don't understand why."

"It's like animals in the wild," Glenda said. "Think of a pack of wolves. The alpha wolf asserts his dominance over the pack by demonstrating his superiority. He leads because the other wolves want him to. Without a leader the pack can't exist."

"But what if I can't?"

"You can, trust me – you can."

# Chapter Twenty-Nine

The hotel was only an hour away from home, close enough to make it an easy drive but far enough to make it feel like they were away. Nate reserved two nights in a suite rather than a regular room. The resort had a nice spa where they could get massages and enjoy the hot tub. In addition to the coffee shop there was a very nice steakhouse on the premises. They left home in midmorning only to find their room wasn't ready when they arrived. With at least an hour to wait, they decided on an early lunch. The hotel coffee shop wasn't crowded since it was well after breakfast but not quite lunchtime. They were both eager to begin their adventure.

"So, so close yet so far," Cynthia said.

"Well, you wanted to leave early and get a, um, 'head' start."

"Funny. At least we won't need a lunch break."

"I wasn't planning on any breaks – I brought my 'boner' pills just in case."

"Since when do you need Viagra?" she said. "Nate, I'm so sorry we had to go through this but I'm so happy we're here now."

"A lot of couples go through this but we're going to be just fine."

Cynthia smiled and touched his hand. "I know."

They finished lunch and went to the front desk and were told their room was ready. Declining the offer of a bellhop, Nate carried their one bag as they took the elevator to the sixth floor and found the room. He put the keycard in the slot, waited for the green light then opened the door. He held it to let Cynthia walk past him.

"Oh my God, this is so nice!"

Nate walked in and had to agree. There was a separate bedroom, a nice living room area, a small kitchenette and dining table. The furnishings were traditional style and very nice. Overall it felt like the upscale room it was supposed to be. Cynthia walked through the living area and toward a sliding door which she opened and stepped through and returned seconds later.

"There's a balcony! I always wanted to fuck on a balcony!"

"After dark, of course."

Cynthia grinned. "Maybe...maybe not."

Nate shook his head as he smiled, he knew he was in for a wild weekend. He went into the bedroom and placed their bag on the king bed and opened it. There wasn't much in it because they wouldn't be going anywhere. He put the few items in a dresser drawer and put the toiletries in the bathroom. Cynthia followed him in and immediately checked out the oversized whirlpool bathtub. She rummaged through the toiletry bag and found her bubble bath at put it by the tub. She walked back to the bedroom and Nate followed her. They embraced and kissed as he ran his hands over her back. His hand started to caress her left breast but she grabbed it and pulled him to the bed. She pulled back the bedspread and the sheets without taking her eyes off of him.

Nate started unfastening the buttons of her blouse as she kicked off her shoes. He pulled his shirt over his head and tossed it aside as she opened his pants. They finished undressing each other and climbed into the bed. They kissed for a long time before he started moving to her neck and breasts. Just as he started moving lower she stopped him.

"I need you inside me...it's been too long."

Nate straddled her and she grabbed his cock to guide him into her pussy. He slid in and felt the wet warmth and started to move.

She stopped him. "Stay still, I just want to feel you for a minute."

Nate just held her. He felt her muscles contract around his cock as he looked at her

He saw her eyes moisten as a tear fell from one corner. He wiped it away with his finger as more started to fall.

She smiled as she cried. "I'm so happy! God I missed you."

Nate started rocking gently understanding that she didn't need to cum, she needed to reconnect. He kept going until he ejaculated quietly a couple of minutes later. She rolled on her side so he could spoon her so he put his arm around her and held her tight. Cynthia fell asleep and he dared not move for fear of ruining the moment. About thirty minutes later she stirred, stretched and rolled onto her back.

She smiled at him. "You may eat me now."

For the next two days they had sex every way imaginable as well as a few variations they hadn't thought of before. There was plenty of oral, different positions of intercourse, he ate her ass and she even ate his a little. They even did a little anal, though he was always afraid of hurting her that way. Just after dusk that first night she fulfilled one wish.

Nate watched as Cynthia slipped on a robe and left the bedroom. He put on his robe and followed her. She was out on the balcony leaning on the railing overlooking the nighttime sky as the sun set. He came up behind her and slipped his hands around her waist. They stayed that way until the sun had completely set. Cynthia turned around and put her arms around his neck. He leaned down and kissed her. She opened his robe and reached for his cock. Despite having ejaculated four times already he quickly started getting hard. She dropped to her knees and started sucking on him. When he was fully erect she stood up and let her robe fall to the floor. She turned around and leaned on the railing bent at the waist with her legs spread slightly.

"Fuck me real slow."

Nate came behind her while stroking his cock to keep it hard. He slipped it into her wet pussy and started thrusting very slowly. She got a sense of his rhythm and started moving with him.

"Mmmm...yeah that's nice."

They rocked like that for a long time. Nate just looked out over the view of the expanse of the valley in the distance. He moved just enough to stay hard. Neither one of them came and that wasn't the point. He felt as if they were one being, alone in the universe. It was the feeling he'd been waiting for the whole time.

The following day they had a round of morning sex and then ordered a room service breakfast. Nate jumped in the shower quickly while they waited for it to arrive. When he was finished Cynthia jumped in for a quick rinse herself. He heard the shower turn off and his wife moving around in the bathroom. A minute or so later there was a sharp tap on the door. He answered it to find a pimply-faced kid in a hotel uniform with a room service cart. He held the door for him to walk past and move the try to the dining table. As he did Cynthia walked out of the bathroom with a towel wrapped around her head – and nothing else. The kids jaw dropped as she just stood there nude, making no effort to cover up. Nate signed the check as the kid stammered his thanks and hurried out of the room. Cynthia was howling with laughter and he couldn't help but join in.

"You trying to give the poor kid a heart attack?"

Cynthia wiped her eyes. "Did you see the look on his face?"

"He probably creamed his pants."

"Probably wondering what that black stuff is between my legs, he'll probably ask his friends."

"They won't know either, these kids have never seen pubic hair. They don't know what they're missing."

They laughed their way through breakfast at the poor kid's expense. Cynthia told him she had no idea what made her do it, she just acted on impulse. When she walked into the room she didn't know whether the server was young, old, male or female. He assured her it was fun and was not at all upset that she did that. She had a spectacular body and it was okay if she wanted to show it off a little.

After breakfast they decided to work on the project Glenda had given them. Nate had a stack of blank paper, two fine point sharpies and a pair of scissors. Cynthia cut the paper into equal size pieces about three inches square. When she was done she handed half the stack to him. He recalled Glenda's instructions and confirmed with Cynthia that he had it right. He was just as excited as when she explained it to them:

> You are to create fifty scraps of paper, twenty-five each. Each of you is to write down every sexual act you can think of. It can be a variation or even some sort of fetish. It doesn't have to be something you like, or have even done, just something you're aware of. Do not tell your partner what you wrote. This means that you may each wind up writing the same thing, that's okay. Each of those pieces of paper should be folded and placed into a jar.

Once a month you will each select a piece of paper, you may wish to have one of you pick on the first and the other on the fifteenth of the month. You will also have another jar with ten scraps of paper, five say 'give' and five say 'receive.' Before your 'date night' the designated person selects the act. At the end of the date the other person picks from the 'give/receive' jar. Then go have fun with it. One note of caution – be careful with your wording to keep it gender-neutral unless you are prepared for the consequences.

It took them almost an hour to complete the task. Nate put the scraps in two small jars they brought along for the project. Despite the amount of sex they'd already had they were both incredibly horny by the time they finished.

Cynthia wanted to take a bath together in the tub so she started the bath water. When it was ready they both climbed in. They sat across from each other and soaked for a bit. After a while Cynthia rubbed his penis with her foot and he used his toe to stimulate her clit. When he was sufficiently hard she straddled him and slid down on his cock. She moved up and down as the bubbles sloshed around them. Nate had ejaculated so many times already that he wasn't sure he could cum again. Cynthia started breathing heavy as she came close to orgasm and this got him excited. He started thrusting as hard as he could in this position and just as she shuddered and gasped he came again himself.

Nate stroked Cynthia's hair as she lay her head on his soapy chest. The water started draining from the tub, she must have opened the valve with her foot. Several minutes later the tub was empty but they held their position and Nate felt himself starting to drift off. Before he was totally asleep he felt Cynthia shift positions. She stood and moved up to his face and brought her pussy forward.

"Eat me!"

He did as he was told and tasted more soap than anything else. She murmured a little and squirmed but didn't really have an orgasm. He was surprised she even wanted it again. After a few minutes she seemed to give up and moved down a little. He tried to help her off of him but she didn't budge. Instead she wiggled a bit which made him a little uncomfortable. He tried to move her but couldn't.

"What are you doing?"

Cynthia grinned slyly. "Marking my territory."

The hot stream hit his chest and a golden river flowed down to his penis.

# About the Author

J.W. Richard is a freelance journalist and graduate of the University of Nevada Las Vegas. Originally from New York, J.W currently resides in Las Vegas, Nevada.

www.jwrichard.com